The Pleasures of a Futuroscope

The Pleasures
of a Futuroscope

Lord Dunsany

Edited by S. T. Joshi

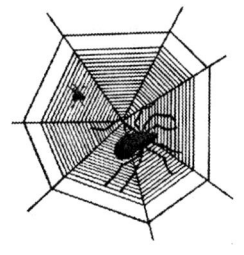

Hippocampus Press
New York

The Pleasures of a Futuroscope copyright © 2003
by The Trustees of the Lord Dunsany Will Trust.
This edition copyright © 2005 by Hippocampus Press.
Introduction by S. T. Joshi © 2003 by S. T. Joshi.

Published by Hippocampus Press
P.O. Box 641, New York, NY 10156.
http://www.hippocampuspress.com

All rights reserved.
No part of this work may be reproduced in any form or by any means
without the written permission of the publisher.

Cover art by Jeff Remmer.
Cover design by Barbara Briggs Silbert.
Hippocampus Press logo designed by Anastasia Damianakos.

Paperback Edition
1 3 5 7 9 8 6 4 2

ISBN 0-9761592-8-7

Introduction

In the summer of 1945, as World War II was grinding to its end after six horrific years, Lord Dunsany (1878–1957), pondering a lifetime of worldwide conflict from the Boer War to the battle against Hitler, wrote a series of essays, *A Glimpse from a Watch Tower,* in which he meditated on the cloudy future that awaited Western civilisation. In the very midst of writing those essays, he learned of a cataclysmic event:

> Strange, strange news came to us to-day. We have just heard of the atomic bomb. . . . I think that a new era started yesterday . . . The picture I long have seen in the dark of the future, growing rapidly less dim as our strange age goes by, is the picture of Man grown cleverer than he was intended to be, but yet not clever enough, and destroying himself by his own skill. Now we are like Phaeton, mounting his father's chariot for the first time. Where will the wild horses take us?[1]

It could well be said that the final decade of Dunsany's career was largely devoted to answering that final question.

In a sense, the transience of the human species was a theme to be found throughout the length and breadth of Dunsany's work. In the memorable prose-poems that fill *Fifty-one Tales* (1915) we find many ruminations on the subject, none more poignant than "The Prayer of the Flowers," who complain of the spread of "cancrous cities" and "glaring factories," but whom Pan reassures with the simple words: "Be patient a little, for these things are not for long."[2] This prose-poem makes evident the source of Dunsany's ire at his own species—the

---

1. *A Glimpse from a Watch Tower* (London: Jarrolds, 1946), p. 41.
2. *Fifty-one Tales* (Boston: Little, Brown, 1915), pp. 36–37.

dominance of the machine. Although his late novel *The Last Revolution* (1951), about machines revolting from human control, is not among his better works, it is his most exhaustive treatment of a subject that had obsessed him for decades. Who can forget *The Evil Kettle* (1925), that pungent one-act play in which the young James Watt sees the lid of a boiling teakettle lifting violently up and down and in that moment conceives of the power of steam—and, by implication, the entire industrial revolution? But Dunsany does not stop with this well-known anecdote; later that night, the Devil comes to little James and pulls back the window: "Smoke as of factories rises up covering the entire landscape. The noise and clangour are heard of the twentieth century. The smoke lifts and a factory city appears in all its devilish ugliness, with an unsightly yellow poster in the foreground, on which is written: TAKE MEDICO. THE CURE FOR ALL AILMENTS. SO NICE. The smoke thickens and the city is covered."[3] But Satan conveniently makes James forget this nightmarish vision of "dark, Satanic mills," and so the industrial revolution proceeds exactly along the course that we all know.

"The Ghost of the Valley" brings this entire topos to a fittingly poignant conclusion. A man meets a ghost in a rural valley; there is no horror in the encounter, only pathos as the ghost, who is "little more than a thousand years" old, tells of his imminent departure:

> "Times are changing," it said. "The old firesides are altering, and they are poisoning the river, and the smoke of the cities is unwholesome, like your bread. I am going away among unicorns, griffins, and wyverns."
> "But are there such things?" I asked.
> "There used to be," it replied.

---

3. *Alexander and Three Small Plays* (London: G. P. Putnam's Sons, 1925), p. 122.

But I was growing impatient at being lectured to by a ghost, and was a little chilled by the mist.
"Are there such things as ghosts?" I asked then.
And a wind blew then, and the ghost was suddenly gone.
"We used to be," it sighed softly.[4]

And so we come to *The Pleasures of a Futuroscope*. The seemingly whimsical, even flippant title of this last novel by Lord Dunsany, written apparently in 1955, should not deceive us as to the serious, even grim message it conveys—but conveys with that lightness and delicacy of touch that only Dunsany could manage. Along with *The Last Revolution* and such whimsies as the Jorkens story "Our Distant Cousins," this novel is one of Dunsany's few ventures into science fiction—and like those other works, it is distinctly light on the science. The futuroscope—a device that allows its user to see into the future—and its inventor, Methery, first appeared in "The Two-Way War," the first story in *Jorkens Borrows a Large Whiskey* (1954). The story is of little consequence, although it too displays a concern with the exponentially greater destructive powers of modern warfare brought on by inventions such as the atomic bomb. Dunsany, in tossing off this brief tale, clearly felt that the conception was capable of more extended use. Neither in the story nor in the novel does Dunsany specify the nature of the device that Methery—who is no more than a name in either work—has created; the narrator of the novel, a retired journalist who has borrowed the futuroscope from Methery, is content to use the instrument merely as a means of entertainment, as if it were a somewhat peculiar television set. But what the futuroscope reveals is far from the contrived laughter of the average sitcom or the still more contrived sus-

---

4. *The Ghosts of the Heaviside Layer and Other Fantasms*, ed. Darrell Schweitzer (Philadelphia: Owlswick Press, 1980), pp. 92, 96.

pense of the average action drama. In what could perhaps be considered the first "reality" show, the futuroscope reveals a future whose contemplation we have all sedulously avoided for the past half-century or more: the apocalyptic collapse of human civilisation.

We are here faced with the aftermath of a nuclear holocaust, perhaps no more than a hundred years from the time of the novel's writing, and then a period of four or five hundred more years in which the pitiful remnants of humanity struggle to wrest a difficult life out of an earth that has lost the machines and conveniences we seem to require to keep our technological civilisation functioning. Dunsany focuses on the adventures of a single family and their attempts to feed themselves, to ward off enemies both animal and human, to marry, and so to propagate their kind. With false naiveté Dunsany states that "all I can do is to tell a simple tale about a few very simple people," but he knows that these people, although stripped of radios or automobiles, are far from simple; their thoughts and emotions are the fundamental ones of people close to Nature and in harmony with its rhythms and objectives.

Tellingly, Dunsany makes numerous comparisons between the buffetings this family endures—being chased by wolves and by a "Wild Man" who is on an even more primitive level than they are themselves, struggling to catch fish in the "great London crater" (the result of a nuclear bomb that has annihilated London, with the Thames rushing in to fill in the immense pit that remains), and fighting off the gypsies who have somehow managed to survive the general collapse of civilised society— and the "thrills" experienced only by way of sports, books, radio, or television. His neo-Stone Age clan dwells closer to Nature, and so it accordingly *lives* the thrills that we can gain only at second-hand. More important, as Dunsany explicitly states, it is these emotions that will provide the "material" for the art and literature that may once again emerge if humanity returns to the path of civilisation.

The novel is set very near the region of Kent that formed Dunsany's chief home when he lived in England—Dunstall Priory, Shoreham, Kent. Scholar Mike Ashley, who himself lives in the same area, has remarked:

> Certainly all of the places he mentions exist and spots like the cross on the hill above Shoreham are well known locally. Most of what he describes he would indeed see from his window up at Dunstall Priory, which overlooks the valley of the Darenth and through which the main road, the river and the railway run. Sydenham, which he mentions with the edge of the giant crater, is where the Crystal Palace mast is, and I'm surprised he didn't mention that, because its metal wreckage would be everywhere, I'd have thought. It certainly couldn't be submerged. The Coldrum Stones also exist. It's one of several such stone circles or collapsed barrows in the area. . . . The Darenth Valley remains very attractive, though, all round Shoreham and the hills where this family would have lived.[5]

Ashley goes on to note that Dunsany's mention of the "Long Man of Wilmington" relates to a well-known figure of a "man cut out into the chalk on the side of the South Downs somewhere west of Brighton."[6]

The gypsies who represent the counterfoil to the neolithic family are of interest in themselves. It is difficult to regard them as true enemies, for the narrator himself remarks that they are "an old civilization that had never strayed far from Nature, and which was surviving still among wild and natural things." For Dunsany, these traits are positive ones, and the fact that the gypsies use metal in a small way—a substance

---

5. Mike Ashley, pers. comm. (25 March 2003).
6. Mike Ashley, pers. comm. (14 May 2003).

regarded with sacrilegious horror by the neolithic people—is a minor fault. The quasi-hypnotic effect of the flute playing by one of the gypsies is highly reminiscent of *The Blessing of Pan* (1927), an unforgettable novel in which a young English boy's fashioning of Pan pipes and his subsequent luring away of an entire community to a more natural life up in the hills, serve to symbolise simultaneously the triumph of paganism over Christianity and the triumph of Nature over civilisation. Nevertheless, our sympathies remain with the neolithic clan, for we realise that they have avoided that first, fatal step toward mechanisation that, in Dunsany's view, would lead all humanity in a "wrong direction"—a direction that would lead once again to James Watt, steam, television, and the atomic bomb.

The Pleasures of a Futuroscope is unique in Dunsany's corpus in many ways: in its remarkable focus on a single "primitive" family's doings over only a few days; in its virtually total reliance upon pure narration and exposition as opposed to dialogue or character development; and in its bold envisioning of a future that initially seems appalling—for surely the destruction of civilisation can be nothing less—but that gradually comes to appear more and more appealing. That Dunsany could produce a novel so compellingly readable with such sparse "materials" is a tribute to his literary gifts; but in truth, its readability comes from the philosophic vision that is infused in every word of the narrative—a vision that sees dangers and evils in the mechanical accoutrements that seem to us so necessary, a vision that suggests our imposing technocratic existence is very far from how Nature intended us to live. As we look around our congested cities, bound fast by highways, telephones, and the Internet, we perhaps have difficulty conceiving that this civilisation could be anything but permanent; and so it is worth considering whether there might be more than a modicum of truth in Dunsany's offhand remark in "The

Policeman's Prophecy": "What a noise we made! But it will all be forgotten."[7]

—S. T. Joshi

A Note on the Text

The text of this novel is derived from a typescript provided by the Estate of Lord Dunsany. It was probably typed by a stenographer, for there are a small number of corrections in pen in Dunsany's hand. I have made no deliberate changes in the text with the exception of introducing some paragraph divisions here and there: in his later prose Dunsany developed a tendency toward immensely long paragraphs, which make for difficult reading. In a few instances I have also made some small changes in spelling and punctuation for the sake of consistency and uniformity.

---

7. *The Man Who Ate the Phoenix* (London: Jarrolds, 1949), p. 95.

The Pleasures of a Futuroscope

Chapter I

Among all the inventions of this age only those have been heard of, let alone used by the public, whose inventors have either had some commercial training or have been in touch with someone who had. Without the help of some such person who understands business, the thing is not put on the market, and there are many inventions today of which no-one knows anything except some clerk in the Patent Office and, so improvident often is genius, that some of these inventions may even have never been patented. Whether they are more wonderful than the ones we know I have no way of telling; but all inventions are wonderful, all of them drawn suddenly by a stray thought out of the absolute void. Indeed in the night around us there must be millions of ideas lurking unknown to man, while thoughts flash out from men like little rare sparks; and the chance of one of those thoughts hitting one of those lurking ideas is probably not much greater than the chance of a meteorite hitting a star. The invention of which I wish to write, so as to introduce its pleasures to the public, is one of these ideas that was hit by the spark of a luminous thought, but the active brain from which the spark shot out was in a lethargic body, or perhaps it is fairer to say that all the energies of that body had gone into the brain; and when the inventor, with the unknown name of Methery, had perfected his invention, the futuroscope, he took no practical steps to get anything from it such as money, and so, if I am so fortunate as to be able to awake any interest of my reader in writing about the futuroscope, he will have to be content merely with that interest, for the thing is not yet on the market, and it is at present what television was a few years ago, a thing known to exist but not in private possession.

The set I have used for the observations to be jotted down in this book I borrowed from Methery, and it is just at present the only set in the world, unless the idea has got out, as ideas will, and the invention has been pirated in some foreign country. That I cannot say. J. H. Methery, of 120 Athenaeum Gardens, a high building devoted to flats, is the inventor and, though the thing is not as wonderful as wireless, of which like television it is a kind of junior branch, and though it would be absurd to claim for him such fame as Marconi's, I think it is only fair that he should at least have been heard of. Many of my friends say No, attaching as much importance to practical success as they do to brilliant inspiration, and holding that, if he is half genius to get the idea, he is half fool to make no better use of it. He did undertake very considerable labour to make the machine and perfect it, though, once he had got the idea, that was not so difficult. But they give him no credit for that, holding that the thing was not complete until it was in the shops and sold at a reasonable price so that it could be as much in the hands of the public as television. I suggested to him that he might have an aerial shaped like a letter M, so as to bring his name before the public, but he said that that was merely silly. And in other suggestions of mine he showed equally little interest, nor would he consult anybody in business who could have helped him far more than I could. Perhaps I can account for his carelessness about business by telling the principal use that he made of his invention, for whenever I saw him use his futuroscope he was turning it on the stars, watching for novas in the remote future and things like that, which shows how little reasonable interest he took in our daily affairs. And when I saw that that lack of interest seemed after a while to extend to his own invention, so that he showed not the slightest keenness about the Derby or the election of the next ten presidents of the United States, I asked him if I might borrow his futuroscope, a practical suggestion that interested him so little that he said he did not think I could easily carry it away. But the moment I suggested a taxi he gave me his permission to take it for as long as I liked. And that is how I came to get a loan of the futuroscope, which I drove out to Kent all the way in a taxi, a bit over twenty miles.

Now to explain its use. It is, as its name is intended to suggest, an instrument for looking into the future, as television looks into distance, each of them bringing the object close to the observer. I say "intended" because Methery's knowledge of the classical languages is no better than that of the man who invented the word "bicycle", so that the name he has given to his machine shows the same ill-assorted mixture of Latin and Greek of which that word is composed; and, for that matter, "television" is no better. When I said to Methery that I would like to suggest a slight alteration he glanced at me with a momentary look of alarm, evidently fearing that I had found something wrong with his instrument. But, when I complained of this bastard word, he lost all interest. And so the thing has to remain as he ill-advisedly named it. It certainly conveys the idea all right; and Methery does not mind how. The thing is rather a camera-like instrument, supported upon a tripod with a black cloth over the top, under which you put your head and look through a thick circular glass the size of the rim of a teacup. There are knobs as on a wireless set, the lefthand one having one letter L, and ten numbers arranged in a semicircle. L stands for Local, and as you turn the knob the other numbers give you other places. By turning the knob you can switch a circle of light pretty well all over England, while another knob, also numbered, moves another circle of flickering light, and is the time-knob. You have to get the two circles together, a mere matter of focus, and the light in the one circle then becomes much brighter and it shows you quite vividly a circular patch of the country at a certain time in the future, according to where you may have twisted the time-knob. Another knob gives you sounds, as with a wireless set, so that you can hear voices there quite clearly, say in a small village in Surrey in the year 2000. Larger than a small village the circle of light will not show very clearly, and even with a small village it is rather dim at the edges; but it can be narrowed and concentrated to a circle of only a few yards across, so that you can see a lawn with daisies on it quite clearly a hundred years hence. It is pleasant to sit with the futuroscope beside me, looking out at the future every now and then and at different parts of the country, just as easily as it used to be to get Vienna or Algiers on the wireless, though for some reason I don't understand I don't find that quite so easy now.

I am no historian, only a journalist, now retired, and living in this small house out in the country, and I no more considered undertaking the enormous work of gathering all the necessary facts which would enable me to write the history of England for the next few hundred years, after which the circular light of the futuroscope tends to grow dim, than I have ever thought, looking the other way, of collecting facts for a history of the last few centuries. I borrowed the futuroscope merely for my personal amusement, very much as people buy television sets. Nor should I dream of using my friend Methery's invention to write anything so serious as a history of England, which is obviously a thing he should do himself. For me to do it would be like reaping another man's cornfield. And so I amuse myself turning that circle of light on the hill in front of my window, and watching its slow changes as I twiddle the righthand knob. At first I see more houses upon its lower slope, where I can remember there being none at all; I turn the knob further over and there are still more of them and higher up the hill, mostly those small ones that we call Council houses, and then I can turn it to a time when they cover the whole hill, all but a part of it on which we have a cross that we cut in the chalk as a memorial to the men who fell in the Kaiser's war. In that far time I saw it stand in a green square left among the houses, with ornamental shrubs at the sides and the cross in the middle. The houses looked so crowded that I soon turned the knobs back to zero, which puts out the light, and I look at the hill through my window instead, and there it is again as I always remember it, with the grass bright in sunlight and the wood dark at the top. I am afraid they are not going to leave much of that wood when they build these houses up to the top of the hill, for I only saw few trees, each standing alone there. And yet I have not said the last word of the wood.

Chapter II

As I have used the futuroscope for my amusement, as most people use television, I find it a little difficult to adapt my discoveries to the interest of my reader, who will naturally look for a more consecutive history of the future than what my random glimpses can afford. If I attempt to place those glimpses in their correct chronological order, I find first of all the increase of small houses, which I have mentioned as covering our hill, spreading like a slow flood pretty well all over England, while roads get wider and smoother. Then I notice cracks in the surface of the roads, and grass and moss, and even scabious, beginning to grow up through them, and growing thicker and thicker, while brambles lean down from the hedges and creep further and further into the wide roads; and I notice about this time that most of the traffic is being done by air. Helicopters are larger then and much improved, and the air seems full of invisible lanes from which no aeroplane deviates. I never knew exactly what date I was looking at, number 10 on the righthand dial of course took me further into the future than number 9, but I did not know what year any of the numbers represented, though no doubt Methery did, but I had not troubled to ask him. I have no scientific or historical purpose and merely use the machine for my amusement, as pretty well everyone does with whatever sets they have.

The further I turned the knob forward from the point at which the wide roads began to crack, the thicker the weeds grew on them and I saw them spread very rapidly, the faintest touch to the knob bringing thousands more, which not only ran out from the hedges but from a wide lawn down the middle of most of the roads which had once been carefully tended and on which I had even seen flowerbeds planted for several miles, separating the two streams of traffic. But now they grew rapidly weedy and only an occasional lorry or mechanized farm-cart ran over the weeds and the flowers, and nearly all the traffic had gone into the air. Trains were still running occasionally, but the railways seemed to have been largely cut out by the roads and, when the roads were cut out by the planes, the railways did not seem to recover their lost ground. But though my vivid circular light could enter houses as easily as television can, I did not find the print of newspapers there very easy to read, so that all the news I got was from the placards outside the shop on which were the headings, or from the wireless in houses which I could pick up with my sound-knob, if the news should be turned on when I peeped into them with my little circle of light, which was quite invisible to the residents there. Building seemed to be spreading everywhere and what we call civilization, and many new inventions of which I knew nothing were constantly being referred to, but it seemed very curious to me, from all the news I could gather by placards or wireless, how little nations change: a certain violent boasting came as of old from Germany, the whole English attitude was still a hope that, violent though the words might be, the Germans were still too good at heart to mean anything by them, and the government that seemed to suit the Russian people best still wavered between the methods of Lenin and the milder government of Ivan the Terrible.

The countryside changed far more than the people. In my own home, with the knob at Local, I see always less of our national trees and more exotic ones, and the wild roses and hawthorn disappearing and giving place to orderly gardens full of flowers which I must admit are more gorgeous than our hyacinths and anemones. And yet I miss the flowers of the woodlands and downs, as the wild slopes where the thyme grows now and the hill-tops on which the hazels shelter anemones shrink to smaller and smaller patches as I peer through Methery's strange instrument into the future. But I must get it into chronological order, which is not so easy, as I have been twiddling the knob to amuse myself with stray glimpses in no particular order. Well, the first thing I noticed was that hedges were disappearing fast from the farms, and this seemed to mean fewer birds, as they had nowhere to nest on the farms, and that meant more insects, and so I saw them using poisonous sprays to protect their crops from the insects, and that of course began to kill the surviving birds that ate the insects, for I soon saw far fewer of them, and before I had twiddled the knob to what I guessed was about a hundred years ahead I could see no partridges at all on any farm wherever I ran the little circle of light, and, seeing none at all after that, I decided that partridges must have become extinct. In this I found out afterwards I must have been mistaken and a few pairs must have survived in what was left of the woods, for much later I saw the coveys all back again and, indeed, more than I had known in my time, which is now. But pheasants had soon quite gone with the gamekeepers and with the large country houses, which soon only survived as museums and ruins and dead places like that. I noticed that singing birds also had greatly decreased, whether by the removal of the hedges in which they nested, by which farmers gain a few more hundred square yards to plough, or because of the great increase of the birds which gamekeepers used to call vermin and which feed on the singing birds.

And then I saw more fog in the country than what I used to remember, and at first I thought it was something wrong with the glass of the futuroscope; but I cleaned it with chamois leather and the fog was still there and someone seemed to have poisoned the fog; for, though of course I could not smell it through the futuroscope, I saw people putting their handkerchiefs to their mouths and noses and coughing, and on one or two occasions I saw elderly people unaccountably drop dead. It was a strange experience glancing through hundreds of years as I was able to do, so that it was easy to notice, to see a civilization growing more and more wonderful, with the air conquered and the earth subdued by pavement, while the people who made this wonderful civilization grew more and more childish. And yet I should not say that, because this people had made this civilization that at many points was too intricate for my understanding. It was more like seeing a very learned professor playing childish games or doing silly things. For instance their rice was still a deadly white as in our time, and the last windmill seemed to have gone, and their flour was fine and white as powdered chalk, and for nearly a hundred years the shades of electric light in some houses were still upside down, as they mostly are in ours. And much else I might have found to criticize had I looked forward in a critical spirit; but I have not yet ceased to wonder at wireless, or indeed any of the great inventions of our time, so that I looked at Methery's little invention only with wonder and gazed at the future in a spirit of awe.

Well, then, what I chiefly saw was a tide of houses setting in from London and all flowing eastward and southward over Kent, while through it like currents ran great roads, wider than any we know, which swept the hedgerows away and sometimes whole fields, until the aeroplanes swept the traffic away and road above road through the sky was as full of traffic as our solid roads are now. The vast increase of the houses naturally narrowed the farms, which I saw dwindling every time that I moved the knob forward, in spite of the trivial gains that they got by destroying the hedges; and, were it not for huge blocks of flats, running even to forty stories, there would probably have been no country left at all, and I began to wonder if there were any countrymen; for the dwellers in those high flats seemed somehow removed from an understanding of the countryside and to be no longer a part of it. The enormously increasing population and the narrowing farms and the greatly widened roads all naturally suggested great import of food from abroad, and such glimpses as I had when, by twisting the lefthand knob, I ran the circle of light down to some of the ports seemed to verify this.

Once I turned the futuroscope on the country by night and the whole land seemed to be twinkling, and it appeared to be more crowded than even it did by day. And after one of these glimpses some way ahead, I came to the conclusion that Nature was finished, and finally conquered by Man. I mean Nature as we know it, woods, hedges and flower-clad hills, and I thought it had been replaced by pavement, houses, roads and machinery, as the Anglo-Saxons replaced the red Indians in America. So foolish a fancy is to be explained, or at least excused, by what I saw when I looked through the futuroscope, with which I frequently played when I had nothing else to do, for all the flowers and grass on the hillside at which I look from my window were gone, except for the little square about the cross, and the woods had disappeared but for a few trees, and I never saw an animal that was not in subjection to Man after the last of the partridges had vanished, except for hawks and magpies and grey crows, and I suppose there were mice and rats on which they fed; and it seemed to me that great roads and fast machines, and electric light which was twinkling from countless windows, were all over England for ever. Reason too seemed to support this fancy, for often enough I had calculated, and heard others calculate, that if a certain invention or achievement of science had advanced so far in so long, it would get so much further in a hundred years and double that distance in two hundred. So I thought that Nature was finished and that the might of mankind dominated the earth. We have little doubt about that might now, but after all those glimpses through the futuroscope it seemed an absolute certainty.

Idle although my purpose was in borrowing the futuroscope in order to amuse hours that would otherwise have been spent in looking out of the window at a scene with less changes than what I could bring to it by twiddling the righthand knob, I had nevertheless one purpose of almost a serious nature, which neither historian nor scientist might consider beneath his notice, and that was to study the increase of the power of Man, by noting the number of new inventions that appeared in a year, and examining the bright buildings to which they gave rise, even where I could not understand their purpose. Indeed I could not understand any of them, so that no temptation arose to rob some man whose grandparents were not yet born, by patenting one of these inventions myself, for they were altogether too marvellous for my comprehension and utterly beyond it, so that it is not much use my attempting to describe them and far less to explain their use. And this will hardly disappoint my readers, for I am afraid that they could not expect me to explain even the wonders of our day or, for that matter, many of the commonplaces. Let anyone try, himself, to explain to a nomad of the Northern Sahara the manufacture and use of a small wireless set; and by use I do not mean so much how it works as why; and he will see at once, however well he understands the dialect of Arabic in use under the Djebal Aures Mountains, what a difficult task it is; and this when he has only to describe an instrument in such common use that the nomad might easily see one if he ever came to a town. Far harder would it be for me, as may be readily understood, who understand nothing of wireless (though a set is within a few feet of me as I write), to explain any of the marvels of transport, bridging and architecture that only I have seen and of which I comprehend so little.

It is no mere selfish wish to preserve these wonderful sights for merely my own amusement that prevents me from describing the strangeness and the magnificence to which the cities of Man had risen, but merely inability to do so intelligently. And when I say the cities of Man I might rather say one city, for wherever I ran the circular light of the futuroscope over England I saw at least one street of continuous houses that joined it all up with London. And purely for my own amusement I did not content myself with the palatial magnificence of the great city I saw, but calculating by the steady growth the futuroscope showed me, I used to prophesy to myself the height to which this city would rise from the earth in another few hundred years, and even found it quite possible to calculate from the basis of things already observed how long it was likely to be before they would bridge the Channel. And then came the day when, twiddling the righthand knob and keeping the left one at Local, I was peering as usual at what had been our village, and which was now a town rambling all the way to London, and looking at the headlines of news, which were still to be seen on placards outside shops, and listening to occasional wireless and noticing with some satisfaction that our relations with Russia still remained good, and even better than they are today, and just as I was about to turn the light of the futuroscope off, there came a flash the whole length of the horizon in the direction of London, which went half way up the sky with what looked like one flame. And after that I was not able to see clearly for some time and a doctor said that water, which repeatedly ran from my eyes, was slightly radio-active.

When I did go back to the futuroscope again, where it still stood in my window, with the lefthand knob at Local and the righthand one at the same number, I moved that knob the merest fraction forward, to see what happened after that extraordinary flash. It was a warm summer's day and must have been about midsummer, for all the may was over, what little was left of it in that urban valley that was such pure countryside once, and on what remained of the farms that had grown so hostile to hedges, and the elder was in full bloom and the wild roses were out, wherever they had escaped the conquering hand of Man. Houses and hills were glittering in bright sun, but I only caught that hot sunlight just in time, for very soon after I had turned the futuroscope on, a dark cloud came in the east and rose up the sky very rapidly and was soon hovering over all the valley.

And then it began to snow. I was just turning the circular light of the futuroscope on to the landscape beyond our valley to the West, which seemed very queer to me, but before I could look at it further the snow blotted out everything. Huge flakes were falling, bigger than any that I had seen before. I watched a man who was hurrying back to the village, that had become a town covering the whole of the hillside, and he acted queerly, trying to brush each snowflake hastily from him, not so much as though he were chilled, but as though the flakes burned him, and I got the idea that they might be radio-active. The houses,

I may say, were still standing; but that great flash I had seen along the western horizon, and which had almost been too much for my eyes, seemed to have shaken them a great deal and, so far as I could see anything through the snowstorm, it seemed that that frightful snow was piling up on them rapidly, and, watching the strange scene anxiously for an hour and getting glimpses of the houses through occasional gusts in the storm that swirled the snowflakes away, I got the idea that the storm was breaking the shaken houses down by sheer weight. The man I had seen hurrying towards the ruins who appeared to be burned by the snowflakes was the only human being I could see in the whole of the landscape, though whether they had been killed by the shock of that flame I had seen go up the western sky, or whether the snowflakes obscured them or they were hiding inside the ruins, I could not tell. But that life had been brought to a standstill there, if not even extinguished, I had no doubt, for I saw a news-placard that no-one had moved still standing outside a shop before the snow began to fall, with a headline on it saying Relations With Russia Satisfactory. Then I saw the one man fall down in the snow, whether burned or chilled I could not tell, and he was almost immediately covered up where he fell among the wild roses. I could do nothing; I was some centuries away from him.

Chapter III

It had been my purpose to study the architecture of the great cities of our future and the marvels of their inventions; but after that astounding flash and the snowstorm my sole interest was in trying to find out what had happened, and, when I found that my knowledge of science was insufficient to understand it, I concentrated for so long as I kept the futuroscope in my house on the simpler work of watching what occurred, or rather I should say what is to occur, in England after that. So I moved the righthand knob, the time-knob, only slightly forward, and never moved it backward any more beyond the point at which the snowstorm occurred, keeping the place-knob almost always at Local, till I came by a knowledge of the Darenth valley that I was tempted to think was unique, till I remembered that there were many who, studying its history backwards, had watched it for far longer than my few centuries, not to mention those who had gone beyond history back into archeology and even geology, to come upon the traces of ways of life whose simplicity I had always associated with the past.

Well, that snow fell for several days, the black cloud that it came from entirely obscuring the sun, and the huge flakes hiding any glimmer of light that might have flickered through. And when the black cloud went and all the snow was flashing in the bright sun of midsummer I saw from its low mounds before it melted that the town was completely destroyed, and when by an almost imperceptible turn of the knob I passed away a few hours I found it even worse than the mounds of snow had indicated; for the shock of the strange explosion must have brought down all the ceilings and so shaken the walls that they had been unable to support the weight of that enormous snow. There lay the valley that I had known, which had become a town and crawled over the hills to join up with the palaces that had crept out street by street from London, all now a heap of ruins. As it was a very hot summer the snow had soon melted, but a curious absence of life, even of mice, all over that swollen village made me suspect there was something bad in that snow, and this I have confirmed as I sit by my window, looking frequently through the futuroscope and turning the time-knob very slowly forwards till I have passed a few years away and find still no sign of life coming back to the ruins, so that I am forced to the obvious conclusion that the whole village is radio-active.

Then I turned the light to see what had befallen the rest of England and, as I suspected from the direction of that great flash, I find the worst is in London. Indeed the downland I look at when I keep the knob at Local is just outside the edge of the great crater, which seems not only to include the whole of London but, stretching across West Kent, to go into Berkshire and to extend its terrible circle far into Surrey and Hertfordshire. This is what I shall refer to as the great London crater. But, running the circle of light controlled by the place-knob over England, I found several more such craters, giving England so much the appearance of the moon, that I wondered if something of the same kind had happened there. At these other craters I only glanced cursorily, then concentrated all my interest on the edge of the North downs that I can see from my window, and see also through the futuroscope, but how strangely altered. Two things, indeed, had altered it, civilization which had destroyed the wild roses and buried the thyme under streets, and then this frightful disaster which had overthrown the houses and was at last to bring back the wild roses. But it was some years before anything grew. And then one Spring, with a strong wind blowing for some days up from the sea, grass, moss and brambles and convolvulus seemed to run back to their own again, and the harsh and desolate lines of the broken walls became all at once dim with greenery. This was certainly not the future for which I had borrowed my friend's strange instrument to observe. But I cannot choose what is coming and I sometimes doubt if any man can, and so, far indeed as it is from anything I set out to see, I have turned all my attention to watching what the future will bring to this valley that lies so peaceful before my window now, though somewhat scarred by old wounds. I did not have to turn the knob very far to see Nature rushing back with all her wild roses, her thyme and the thousand tendrils of her convolvulus to the hill from which she had been so long exiled by civilization and by disaster.

One day I saw a fox on the edge of the woods on the hill, and next day penetrating further into the wood I saw a badger, and these two things gave me the hope that men had also survived. And the hope was justified, for turning the time-knob some way ahead, with the place-knob always at Local, I saw at last a young fellow walking along the side of the hill, stepping over the ruins without taking any notice of them and going to his home, which I was just able to make out at the very end of the hill. I had been so long expecting to see men housed in towering palaces, since first I borrowed the futuroscope, that I almost missed the home that this young man entered. And it was not easily distinguishable from the rest of the domain of Nature, whose reign appeared now so absolute, quite unchallenged by Man, or by that revolted slave that became his master, the iron creature whose veins held petrol or steam. The roof of the house was of thatch, the walls were of logs and the windows were very small and without glass. The chimney was built of rocks joined by some sort of clay and ran straight down to what, judging from the outside, was a large fireplace.

It seems easy, when one is given this rare opportunity to peer into the future, to tell simply what is coming, and it might be to some, but so vast was the vision which this strange instrument showed me, that I found the greatest difficulty at the outset in telling a coherent story at all. To begin with I had nowhere near enough knowledge of science to know what had happened when that flame lit all the horizon or to know what made such an explosion possible, any more than I ever knew just what happened upon the moon. And then I saw before me, wherever I looked, a scene to describe which adequately I should need the training of a botanist and more knowledge of wild life than comes our way anywhere under the reign of civilization. So what I decided to do, in order to tell anything of this strange future at all, was to ignore the forests and marshes of the great London crater and all the other craters and the green land and the forests in between them and observe the story of one of the inhabitants of this land that I knew so well and which was so strange to me, some young man such as the one whom I had seen walk into the reed hut and close the heavy door behind him; but rather one of his descendants than he, for I wanted to see how men would deal with the times to be brought by the strange commotion that I had witnessed for a moment, before the flash dazzled my eyes. The history of the next few centuries, the altered geography of the country, the great explosion itself and the cause of it, I will leave entirely to Methery.

Chapter IV

As soon as I had had my breakfast next day I went to the futuroscope, as my custom is, and turned on the righthand knob, five or six hundred years from the time I had first seen a man after the disaster, whatever it was. I turned the light full on the same part of the hill as where I had seen the hut, and was surprised to find it still there, or another one built or the same spot. Not much had greatly altered. The woods along the top of the hill that I knew, which had been swept away as the village increased to a town, had all come back again. The farms that the town had so nearly overrun were almost all gone again, this time being covered by forests, but the slopes of the downs were much as they used to be: thyme was still growing upon them in bright patches and bushes of wild roses, and they had evidently been kept clear for the grazing of sheep. I was so far ahead now that I was able to form some idea of the destiny of Man, though whether it goes in waves, from barbarism to the height of a civilization and to barbarism and civilization again, or whether what I saw is indeed the lot that was intended for Man in the beginning, and to which after straying awhile he will come again, I could not tell, for the futuroscope soon goes dim after the time to which I turned the knob after breakfast this morning.

To understand this more clearly I decided to enter the hut with my circular light, which it does as easily as the scenes of television enter one of our houses. So, moving the broad circle of light up to the hut, I contracted it by twisting the knob which controls the size of the circle and looked inside. And there I saw a family, a man and his wife and three children, or rather a son who was just grown-up and a boy and a girl who were nearly so. They were dressed in skins and a rough cloth. But what gripped my attention at once and interested me more than anything else that I saw was the complete absence throughout the whole of the hut of any sign of our civilization. There was no relic of it there whatever. We might not even have been. Why, I had collected myself fossils from the chalk and from the gault which lies two strata below it, and have sometimes picked up a flint axe-head in clayey fields that lie on top of our downs, so I have records of many past ages in my house; but of our own age here there was nothing. And by that I mean that there was no trace of anything man had made since he had abandoned flint and had discovered iron. There was pottery, there were woven wool, there were plaited rushes, there were sawn planks and cut beams; but all the implements that could have cut them and sawn them which I saw in the hut were of flint, good sharp flint as though man had never emerged from the stone age nor heard of iron or bronze. This meant of course that there were no iron bars in the grate and that the fire which was burning there was of logs heaped on the hearth. And there were no latches for doors or windows except of timber. This astonished me very much, for I knew that the country must contain many thousands of miles of rails, as well as fallen factories and, for that matter, cities.

And then an incident occurred which gave me the clue at once. A younger boy, one of about eight years old, entered the hut while my luminous circle was there in the middle of it and stretching from wall to wall, and he had in one hand the very thing that I missed in the hut, a piece of iron, one of our axe-heads. It was completely rusted all over, but there was no mistaking its shape and it still had an edge of a sort. The man turned sharply towards the boy, with his mouth open, so did the boy's mother, and his sister and two brothers turned their heads at once towards him with obvious surprise. I turned on the sound-knob then and got their words very clearly. "Throw it away," said the boy's father sternly, and all in the hut were looking at the rusty old axe-head with something like horror. The boy, who had been pleased with his discovery, suddenly lost his delight in it and I had no doubt that he had already been made to see, before I turned the sound-knob on, that he had picked up something shocking, something that should not have been touched. And I saw from all their faces, before I heard their words, that that bit of metal was one of the things over which there was some kind of curse. The father's and mother's exclamations soon left me no doubt of that. Iron and steel I could see were, according to their creed, things that had failed the world, or that led to things that had failed it, and so must be rejected, according to them, as teetotallers reject strong drink on account of the excesses to which it may lead. As we would keep whiskey or gin away from a child, so they angrily compelled this boy to throw the old axe-head away.

That one little outburst explained to me at once why there was no sign of metal, not even of metal nails, in the whole of the hut, and why I saw no sign anywhere of any use being made of all the rails that must be lying under the soil in England in the age to which I had turned the time-knob of the futuroscope. I withdrew the light from the hut and widened it again and swept it over the country, and I very soon picked up marks of the line that runs to Dover. I knew roughly where to look and, whenever I got clear of forest, I soon saw lumps in the grass whose straightness showed me they were artificial, as well as stains of a slightly different colour which still marked the fields, just the old craters of Hitler's war did still, most of them long ago filled in, although some were little dells giving shelter to primroses. It is curious how this one little incident gave me the clue to the whole philosophy of these people, and everything I heard them say afterwards fully corroborated it: it was that timber for firing and building, sheep for eating, flint for working or fighting, clay for pottery, and, in fact, everything else that one saw all over that valley, had been intended for Man and that he had lived accordingly for what they called forever, until the time came when he took what they considered the wrong turning, and that their view was proved to be right by the ruin that this ill-directed cleverness had wrought, and that therefore even to touch anything that had been amassed during that journey down what they considered the wrong road, which had led away from the stone age, was wicked; and I saw that that steel axe-head which the abashed boy had been made to throw away was actually an accursed thing.

The language had not much altered, so that I was able to understand what these people said as soon as my sound-knob was turned on. I was glad to see that Kentish dialect to some extent still survived, though much mixed with the accents that we have come to associate with the B.B.C. One alteration in the language was very much for the better: meaningless phrases that people are supposed to accept today as though they understood them, and which they do so accept, were gone and a lost simplicity had returned. There was also a dog in the hut, whom I heard them call Toby. He was lying contentedly on a deerskin before the fire and looked up gladly when the boy came in, and then rather drooped his head as though he knew the boy had done wrong, more likely by sensing the rebuke that there was in the air of the hut than by anything he knew about metal. Close up against the hut was what was evidently a sheepfold, though the wattled hurdles were higher than any that I had ever seen, and the sheep were grazing between the hut and the wood on the slope of the hill over which I noticed butterflies flying again, though for many years after the great flame and the snowstorm there had been none. They or their forbears must have drifted there on a wind from somewhere beyond the disaster and were now as numerous as they ever had been. Flowers and grass also had withered under that snow, but, wherever the seeds had come from, they were all back again now. Then I turned the futuroscope off in order to have tea, and did not return to it until some while later, when the sun was nearly touching the western hill. Then, with the knobs at exactly the same places, I turned the light on to the hut and found that the sheep had all been gathered in to the shelter of the high hurdles and I wondered why.

It is odd that when I decided to estimate this strange future time, and to try to judge of Man's way through it, by watching the fortunes of one single family, it was their dog that I really got to know first. I cannot say quite what kind of dog he was, but he looked more like an old English sheepdog than anything and was pale grey and white in patches, and his white face between two grey ears and a patch of grey on his forehead had a most kind and lovable expression. And I say this though he showed no liking for me; for, though the luminous disk of the futuroscope was evidently entirely invisible to everyone in the hut and never alarmed a bird outside, yet the dog seemed always aware of the presence of something whenever I turned it on him, or even if it entered the hut at all, and growled slightly even if he was asleep, indeed as much then as at any time, as though he were troubled slightly by something in the nature of dreams.

But now, as I was looking at the high hurdles, I heard him growl in earnest from the inside of the hut, and, running the light back into it, which, as I have explained, was as easy for it to do as it is for television, I saw him standing with his teeth bared and all his hackles up. The two elder boys and their father all picked up flint axes at once, which, fastened to long rods of hazel, were leaning against the walls, and went outside, the dog running in front, growling all the time, and I followed them with the circular light to the sheep-hurdles. I could see nothing, nor, I think, could the man and his two sons, but the dog could, for he turned to where some long grasses waved for a moment and began barking angrily. It was evidently the first wolf coming down in the twilight, for I caught the word "wolf" said by the boys; though how a race now extinct in England could have come back I did not know, but assumed that Alsatians and others that they had bred with had gone back to something much like one of the breeds of wolf that inhabit certain parts of Europe today. Presently the dog stopped barking, and then they all went back into the hut, some faint ejaculations coming occasionally from the dog's lungs, as though he had a few barks left over for which there was no longer any need. I ran the light along the edge of the wood and even into it, but daylight was fading away and the pale light of the futuroscope could not brighten the wood, and I saw nothing, so I moved it back to the hut. And there I saw, almost from the way that they put their axes down and from the way that the dog curled himself up at once in front of the fire, that the business of keeping off a danger from the sheep was no more than routine. And yet the dog remained watchful, with head raised, and all in the hut had an expectant air as though they waited for something more.

I stayed a long time that evening looking through the futuroscope, for it chanced to be evening with me as well as round that rude hut so far in the future, and I kept the sound-knob in position so as to learn as much as I could of their way of life, and in particular what they feared, as the twilight faded away in the valley and the darkness moved down from the wood. I heard them speak again of wolves, and then the woman and her daughter went to another room and I heard what sounded like the washing of pottery dishes and other sounds of household work, and one of the boys began to make a bow and the other sat chipping a spearhead out of a flint. And the man sat down by the fire and began to work at something so minute that I could not pick it up with the futuroscope, but I saw him striking with a flint at what I took to be a small flake which he had struck off another flint, and then he began filing it with a rougher stone, and it was not till I saw him fasten it to a thread, or more likely a dried sinew of some small animal, that I guessed that what he had been doing was making a fishhook. It was quite dark by then outside the hut, and the interior was lit by rushes burning in tallow and by the glow of the fire. The dog Toby was fast asleep, and then in an instant he was wide awake, with his head up listening intently, and shortly after that I heard the howl of a pack hunting, and the man and the two boys picked up their stone axes again. This time they did not go out, but waited, listening, all three of them and the dog; and the hunting cries came nearer and nearer still, till they were quite close to the sheep. I had rather wondered why in midsummer, as it was then, they had a fire on the hearth, but I saw the reason for it now, for each of them picked up a burning log and went out of the hut with Toby, with an axe in one hand and a burning log in the other, and before I could follow them with my luminous disk I heard the note of the wolves, or whatever they were, change as they evidently turned from the flaming logs and went on to hunt elsewhere. I heard a stern shout to Toby, and then all four came back into the hut with the burning logs left outside and the man shut the door again and ran two wooden beams into sockets to hold it. So much care he took in fastening them that I wondered why such stout beams shot into sockets hollowed out of the trunk of a beech were needed to keep out wolves or overgrown wild Alsatians. Furthermore the man stood listening, anxiously as I thought, even after the wolves were gone, as though he feared something else, and I could not think what. The longer I looked, the more that apprehension seemed to increase. Nothing at all was said, and I could only guess by their faces and by the attitude of the dog that they feared something, and by the time I had to turn off the light in order to have my supper I could not make any guess as to what it was.

Chapter V

As I sat at my supper I thought much of the progress of Man, his amazing cleverness, the practical use to which he put it, the enormous power of his machines, their rapid increase, and the power and might of the civilization that increased with them; till I perceived how what I had actually seen was a certainty (though, had I not seen it, I should never have guessed it) that it was not Man that was growing more powerful, but only the machinery he had invented; so that, the more wonderfully it grew, the sooner that iron infant of his must grow beyond his control, and when it did so, being helpless without him, it must all break to pieces. But these are idle thoughts.

And, turning soon from mere speculation on the rise of Man, if it be a rise, from the simple course apparently intended for him and back in a few thousand years to that course again, to the few things I could observe with my own eyes, I hurried back to the futuroscope and turned the light on the inside of the hut, where all the inhabitants of it had still, as I thought, a certain strained air of attention. And scarcely had I turned on the sound-knob and focussed it to the right time, when I heard a hoot from the hill ringing down from the woods and yelling all along the valley and echoing away down the Darenth where the night had been all silent; and, before it could become silent again, another yelling hoot ripped through the night. That was the noise they had evidently been waiting for, and the man dragged the heaviest log that lay beside the fire and shoved it against the door, which was already barred with two beams. It was too dark for me to see anything on the hill outside the hut and I could only judge by the sound, and the sound puzzled me. There was, shall I say, the note of it and the tone of it. The note had a human accent, but the tone was so wild that one thought of a wild beast; yet I could not think what beast, or how it could have got into England. I listened for some time before I heard it again, and then it was far away, so that whatever it was, it moved swiftly.

I know that a historian, if he had an instrument such as I had the loan of, would plan his observations very carefully, though I do not know how; and a scientist would make observations more carefully ordered still, and again I do not know what his methods would be and I suppose they would depend on what branch of science he followed. But I, I must admit, only followed whatever chanced to catch my ear or eye or awake my curiosity, and now my interest had been caught by this family behind the barred door of their hut with the night all round them, and strayed a little away from them, guided by curiosity to see what this great voice was that went bellowing through the night, and I followed it over the hills until I lost it. It was strange to be following thus some dangerous creature in perfect safety. And that is one of the pleasures of the futuroscope. A glance at the faces of all in the hut, the man barring the door with the big log as well as the two beams, the hackles all rising on the neck of the dog, the two elder boys clutching their axes, and the wondering look on the face of the girl, all told me the thing was dangerous; but, like someone watching by television some harrowing tragedy that wrings no tears from him, so with ear and eye I followed this dangerous creature all through the woods and the night, but failed to come up with it. My curiosity still unslaked, but at least satisfied that the danger had passed from the family in the hut, I turned off the futuroscope then, and with all its knobs back to zero I returned to my own affairs and our own time and put my cat out and went to bed.

 I live very much alone in this small house of mine, having retired from the profession of journalism and having left London twenty miles and several years behind me. My cook comes in three times a day from a cottage not far off and a charwoman comes up from the village twice a week, and it is seldom that anyone else comes in, so that my futuroscope excites no more attention in my sitting-room than it has in the larger world. If anyone asks what it is I say a new kind of television, which satisfies every questioner, for television is still too new for anybody to know what varieties are still being put on the market. The scenes that it shows are of course only observed by me when I turn the knobs and put my eye to the peephole, and the ones that sometimes ring from the future through my house are no stranger than what one may hear from a thriller that may be broadcast, or even from atmospherics. I now kept the lefthand knob always fixed at Local, or rather infinitesimally to one side of it, which brought the light right on to that hut, while I had the righthand knob at exactly the same spot in the future. All I had to do then was to switch on the futuroscope, by which I mean connect its batteries with the electricity of my lighting system, and I was looking right into that cottage, and when I turned on the sound-knob I could hear all they said. It is as simple as that. I think I shall feel rather lonely when I have to return the set to Methery, and I am saving up to buy a television set when that time comes.

It was one of the days when the charwoman does not come up from the village, and I had several things to attend to to keep my house tidy, so that I did not think of turning on the futuroscope all day. But when evening came and the birds had stopped singing and the light was growing dim, the sound of a dog barking across the valley caught my attention and somehow set me wondering how things were going with that family in the hut on a slope of this very valley, or perhaps I should say how things were to go with them in about five hundred years' time, though I find it difficult, as I look through the glass and see those people vividly in the circle of light that the futuroscope casts on their hut, to realize that they are not all moving and speaking today and that they and I can never be contemporaries. So I switched on the light and they were all in their hut, barring the door again and leaving their stone axes against the wall, as though they had just come back from scaring off another wolf from their sheep, whose baaing outside the hut my sound-knob was picking up. Then they all sat down before their fire and began eating their supper, with far better bread, I am sorry to say, than ours, and what looked like very good cheese. They spoke little during their supper, but it was then that I began to pick up their names, and much to my surprise they were all names that I recognized; not that I ought to have been surprised, for I was much nearer to them than we are to the Norman conquest and we still have plenty of names like William and, for that matter, many that are much older, such as Alexander and Julius. The elder boy was called Bert, and the second one Alf, and the name of the girl was Liza; and I heard the woman call the man Joe, and he called her Maud, and I wondered if some influence of Tennyson had drifted down the ages to name her.

And then they were all silent and still, listening to some sound that I had not heard yet; and I too listened, and presently, picked up by the instrument quite clearly, came the wild hoot over the hill. I caught the awe in the eyes of the girl, and the strained attention of all of them, and the man dragged again a big log through the hut and put it against the barred door. An unaccountable impulse came to me for a moment to call out and ask him to wait till I had gone out before he closed up the door. And then I realized, firstly, that I had only to give a most delicate touch to the lefthand knob to change my view of the hut for a view of the valley, and secondly that I was several centuries away from him. But some of our impulses are more swift than our calculations. My circle of light was at once outside the hut and, widening it, I ran it up the valley in the direction of the wild cry where the gloaming had not yet quite gone over to night, against which, as I explained before, the futuroscope's pale circle of light was of no avail. And, just as I began searching, that cry rang out again, weird with an increased volume and much nearer, and I turned the luminous circle straight towards it, but with some apprehension although so many centuries lay between it and me. Then coming so straight towards me that I shuddered, protected though I was by the years, I saw the huge figure of a man holding in each of his hands a great ashpole, as I took it to be, with thick dark hair coming down to below his shoulders. So this was what some men had gone back to! I stared with a mixed wonder, wonder at this awful savage figure, and wonder at some odd instinct in myself which told me that I had seen this man before. Not in the future, certainly not in our present. Where then? And it came to me all at once, so that I shouted, and my cook heard me and wondered what I was saying, "The Long Man of Wilmington!"

Yes, it was no more than a day's walk, for a gigantic savage like that, from Wilmington in Sussex; and the thought came to me that someone I may have seen ploughing fields near there, or even some shopkeeper in Hastings, may have been descended from that wild man whose portrait was cut on the hill by the villagers of a hamlet first known as Wild Man's Town, discarding uncomfortable consonants as years went by, and whose descendants had gone back whence they had come. And what a fine defence those two staves must be against wolves or men or anything else, the lefthand one keeping them off and the right crashing down through their bones. He strode swiftly towards me and I moved the little light out of his way as one might step from the path of an elephant. I turned it on him again at once and saw him going right up to the hut, where he laid his hand on the thatch and shook it impatiently, and then moved round to a window, which was much too small for him to enter, and peered inside. He grunted once or twice and then went away slowly. Then darkness came down so thick that I could see no more, and I moved the light back to the hut and contracted it and ran it inside. And the boys were there, holding their axes, and the father seemed to be comforting the girl. But her eyes were turned to the window and were looking away towards the night. A melancholy hoot or roar sounded over the hill, and the Long Man was gone.

Chapter VI

Once more I recommend the futuroscope for the student of almost any branch of man's enquiries. History is an obvious study for anyone who may come into possession of one of those rather interesting instruments, and I have only discarded that study myself because five hundred years or so of the history of England seems a subject altogether too vast for me and would use up all the leisure I had, which I like to enjoy after a life of hard work in Fleet Street; and besides, I am not a historian. And then there are botany or entomology which I might have taken up, for all the slopes of our downs were laid bare to me in any season I liked and at any time of day. And I feel that I might have made some contribution to science, had I been prepared to give up my leisure and had I not been lured, as I have been, to study the story of one family not far removed from the savage, who seemed, at the time that I watched them, to go in fear of someone the other side from them of the line that divides a very crude form of peasantry from the naked savage. I could not observe everything, and this was the bit of the future I chose to observe. Besides which my observations were expensive; for, though I have not mentioned this detail, the instrument has to be connected with the mains, and a very considerable flow of electricity, if flow is the right word, is required to keep objects clearly visible in the luminous circle that the instrument throws on the future, and double the amount is required to operate the auditory part of it. All these considerations limit the scope of my enquiries into the future.

I did occasionally run the disk of light round the countryside, to see the kind of conditions under which the family lived, but mostly I kept it at Local. To the south of them lay the Weald, the sandy country below the chalk and the gault, which was almost entirely forest. Round about them lay the grassy slopes of the downs on which they grazed their sheep, and the tops of all the hills were dark with forest. To the northwest lay the great London crater, a huge circle the Thames had entered making a reedy lake. Willows still lined the Darenth, where I look from my window at their great pollarded heads; but, like man, they had all gone wild, when I turned the futuroscope on them so far ahead, and huge branches grow out of those once neat heads by then and sweep down to the ground or the wide floods of the Darenth. Low down near the Darenth this family lived in that reed-thatched hut, the walls of which were of logs of beech, stout enough to keep out wolves or wild men. And there came to me as I looked at their beechen walls the thought that the folk in that hut were safer than we in our cities, which are altogether vulnerable today to the attack of an enemy, and so remained until the day when that queer flame went up all along the horizon and there fell the heavy snow that ended that summer and all its civilization.

I write of what I saw in the futuroscope, without knowing more of the causes of it than what my guesses can tell me, and I do not regard them as being of sufficient value to give them a place among things I actually saw. It is the quite unscientific and merely human interest that I began to feel in this family which soon caused me to keep the two knobs at the same numbers, so that the illuminated disk was always in or about that hut while I watched their simple story. I admit that anybody who may be fortunate enough to come into even temporary possession of a futuroscope should make more scientific investigations than what I am doing; but one is either born with scientific interests or one is not, and that is my excuse for occupying the leisure hours I spend over this strange instrument with matters of so little scientific value as bits of the life-stories of this crude little family that had somehow slipped back to the edge of the paleolithic age, as all things about them seem to have done. Two fears they had, one of this man with the two great sticks, a few centuries wilder than they, for he seemed to have slipped back quite that much further into the dark of the stone age; the other a fear of anything whatever that remained of the wonders of our time. And from the look of awe that I saw in their faces as they saw that piece of metal that the youngest boy had picked up, I got the idea that if they regarded the wild man as a danger to their family in that hut they feared even the beginnings of those great inventions which have so luxuriantly flowered in our age as a greater peril to the entire race.

I should explain, if I am not being too complicated, that if I left the knobs exactly where they were, then time moved forward over the futuroscope exactly as it does here. And so that is what I did. I mean that, by leaving the time-knob where it was, and of course the place-knob also, I found that, when I returned the luminous disk to the hut twenty-four hours later, exactly twenty-four hours had passed over the hut too. Leaving the two knobs just in their places was therefore a convenience that gave me a consecutive story, and having, as I said, no scientific interests, I was not even tempted to send the luminous disk racing far ahead through the future, nor should I have seen much if I had; for, as I think I have mentioned, it soon tends to get dim after five or six centuries.

Well, then, I returned to the hut again at twilight after I had tidied up everything in my house on my side of the valley, and on my side of all those hundreds of years. As I turned the light on to the hut I waited a long while listening, and so did they, with the three axes near to their hands, and a strange and wondering look on the face of the girl, but no wild man came that night. Perhaps he was far away in Sussex, which I somehow looked on as his native home because he seemed so like to that wild man whose portrait has been carved in the chalk at

Wilmington. One wolf came near the sheep and was soon scared away, and then all was quiet. The dog was asleep, and so alert even in sleep, with his nose between his paws on the deerskin rug, that when I turned the luminous disk on him he gave little sleepy barks, as though there were something akin between this strange instrument and his dreams. And once as the disk touched him he wagged his tail, which old English sheepdogs were never allowed to do in the age from which my sight and my interest had been temporarily withdrawn, and their tails were always cut off in case they should.

Presently they all sat down to supper at a stout table, sawn from the trunk of a beech, with axes leaning against the table beside three of the chairs; and I noticed, what I might have seen from the first moment that I turned the luminous disk on them, that everything was more intense with them than it is with us. There is no excitement for us, however hungry we are, in eating a meal of ground corn and cheese and bacon, but one saw from the good rough grain that one of them must have ground it, not some remote machine, and somebody had grown it, winning it with toil from the hard earth. And there was a fish that one of them had caught, and, looking up from the slices of bacon, I saw sides of bacon and hams high up in the smoke of the fire, and I saw that this supper, like every meal they had, was a climax of successful toil, and not only that, but that it was eaten in a security that they successfully held, however narrowly, against all that roamed in the night and threatened them and their sheep. So that to bring this supper to their table, and eat it without disturbance by any danger from outside the beechen beams that guarded their hut, was the sort of excitement that we get more rarely, as when we watch a finish at cricket or football and just see our own side win. We have our excitements too; we earn money with hard work and spend some of it on going to a cinema, and we watch events as thrilling as any I saw through the futuroscope; but here the excitement seemed all to come more immediately and directly and with an intensity that did not require to be summoned up by alcohol or tobacco, neither of which they had, but which seemed to be there already, needing only the event to stimulate it. There came the far cry of a wolf and they were all alert at once, and stimulated as much as we ever are by a thriller. Then the cry sounded further away and they turned back to their supper, as we might turn from some exciting news in the paper to eat our breakfast. But what toil has gone to provide us with that excitement, which the night and the wolf provided them so directly! I saw no trace in that hut of anything printed or written, and I doubted if anything remained anywhere of all the distilled thought, wonder and yearnings of Man which we call literature. That will be a great loss, but the material will still be there, and was there before me in that luminous disk, the lives of men and women with all their throbbing emotions. It was as though that lovely scent, attar of roses, were no longer in all the world, but roses were still there, so that the scent could be brewed again.

These are merely idle reflections that come to me as I run my eyes along the walls of that hut past the wide pans of baked clay on the beechen shelves, the buckets for water and milk, none of them like our buckets, but made out of goatskins, the saws and spears and axe-heads, all of flint, the deerskin rugs, a bow cut from a yew-tree, a fishing-rod made of hazel, the dog asleep on the floor, but all ready to warn them of danger, and the family enjoying the meal that they had won from the earth, to which they seemed so near, and from which something, I don't know what, seems to be sliding us further and further away. This, then, was the return, the homecoming of Man again to Mother Earth, the return of the prodigal with all his treasure lost, the treasure that the arts have given to all the ages, but a prodigal still able to work, and able, I trust, to find again one day the glory of Greece from which we too have wandered so far.

Chapter VII

I think that in the warmth of that hut I must have fallen asleep, not that I could feel the warmth of it, but I must have felt some sympathy with the drowsiness that I could see gradually coming on all in the hut, as one by one they went to some other room, leaving the dog still sleeping by the fire, guarding them all in his sleep; for I knew that if my invisible and soundless circle of light could stir him, though ever so slightly, there was no doubt that any sound would wake him at once, even though it should come near the door on feet that were soundless to me. If I did go to sleep I don't think I missed anything, for there was no sign on the faces of the people I watched to suggest that any exciting thing had occurred. Then I switched the futuroscope off and went to bed.

My interest in the future had now become localised in this one family in the hut in the valley of the Darenth, an admission that shows me to be no scientist and which will excite the scorn of any historian whose eye may chance to fall on these words, if ever that eye condescends to so trivial a theme. But we do not always choose where our interest falls, and there it was. And having become interested in them I became uneasy with their apprehensions, and wondered what the wild man was doing round there and if he would come again. After breakfast I went to the futuroscope and connected it up with the mains, and there the light was inside the hut again. But only the woman was there, scrubbing pottery dishes and rubbing them with sand and continually going away into what I took to be a store-room for food. These household details not interesting me, I roved the light outside and saw the girl feeding some pigs in a sty just beyond the sheep-pen, which was now empty, and, running the light up the slope of the western hill, I soon saw the man among his sheep. Later I went back to the hut, I mean that I turned the light back; and the girl had returned to the house and I listened to hear where the boys were and what they were doing. My progress was slow there because, unfortunately, I could not say a single word to them to indicate anything that I wanted to know, and, considering that men in London can now talk to Tokio, I think that an inventor ought to be able to do that much. My inability to do it was distinctly inconvenient and I should complain of this to Methery, were it not that it might seem somewhat ungracious of me to make any complaint to him at all when he has lent me a machine from which I have had so much pleasure. However, there it is, and I cannot speak with those people in whose presence I felt I was, and all I could do was to wait for them to speak and to hear what they would say, and to hope that it might be something of interest to me.

What I did hear was that the eldest boy Bert had gone over the hill through the forest with his bow in order to get a stag, and the other two boys had gone off together, but that was all that I heard about them and I could pick up no information as to where they had gone or what they were going to do. None of the boys had taken Toby with them and he was not even out on the hill watching the sheep, from which I saw that his job was always to guard the house, and he lay now just outside the door in the sun, doing so. As I saw no sign of money in the house, it seemed evident that cheese and bread and all the things which that family needed were made by themselves and, as I watched the girl Liza making cheese, I realized that our enormous system of commerce had gone with the fall of snow that followed the flash, and the trivial things that it did not interest me to observe had become of the first importance.

And now I began to see that sports such as hunting and shooting have on our own age the grip which they have because they are planted so firmly in our blood, and that they are planted firmly there because our race could not have survived without them. Our love of sport is an ancestral love that has come down from hunting, and now it was evidently a dominant impulse again, not confined to the fortunate few, but essential to the existence of any. Cheesemaking and milking goats, which I now saw that they possessed as well as sheep, could not interest me, brought up in a commercial system which leaves so much to remote towns, as much as it was interesting Maud and her daughter. So I switched off the current and returned, with some of the shock of surprise that I felt whenever I did so, to so different a scene. If I look out of my window, certain things are the same, though not much, but the shape of the hills is unaltered: it is my room with its wallpaper, its plastered ceiling, its chintzes and, above all, my clock, which are such a surprising change that I can never switch off from that reed-thatched hut without feeling a little shock. I think I mentioned that the time of day synchronized, so that at any rate within a few minutes the time that I was keeping was the same as that which passed over that hut by the Darenth five or six centuries on. At any rate the difference was less then the difference that we make in summer between our clocks and the real time.

I looked at the futuroscope no more that day until some time about sunset and busied myself with various things in my house and my small garden, which are too trivial to have any interest were I to record them, as was the work of the two women in the hut to me. And yet I cannot escape from the feeling that my little tasks are really of no importance, while the work of those two women, trifling though it appeared to me, was of fundamental importance, as would be the work of the boys, whatever they might be doing; and it was to hear where they had gone and to see what luck they had had that I connected up the futuroscope with the mains and looked again at the hut that evening. And there was the hut with the sheepfold beside it and all the sheep shut in, and I sighted the light on the inside of the hut. In the hut I saw the dog and all that family except Bert, the eldest boy, and I saw at once from certain looks of anxiety on all the faces, and even perhaps on the dog's, how intense a life was lived where there were no movies, no thrillers, no stop-press editions of evening papers, but where life was, as it were, raw and contained its own thrills, without the need of any art or research to produce them. Here as they waited for the return of Bert, with his father watching at the open door and all of them straining their ears for any sound, I felt that the atmosphere was like that of the end of a play, while they waited for a denouement that nobody had to distill as the dramatist does from life, but which was provided every day by life itself; and there seemed to be between this life and ours something of the difference that there is between drinking milk from a cow, and eating out of a tin some cheese that was made in a factory. As the gloaming darkened and the boy did not return, that intensity with which not all our plays succeed in thrilling a house, that setting suitable for a tragedy, seemed to increase. And then there must have come a shout from the hill, which I did not hear, and the dog, which had gone to the door, turned back and lay down by the fire, and the man also came in, and said "He has come out of the wood."

Their ears strained a little still to hear if any wolves were pursuing, but there was no sound, and in the relieved tension Bill, the youngest boy, began to tell of his fishing. He had gone with Alf to the edge of the lake that mostly filled the great London crater, and told how he had waded out through the rushes and nearly caught a pike. He told of his walk over the hills with the keenness of a boy, everything vivid and beautiful to his eyes at that early age, and in what looked like the early age of the earth, where you would not notice that its dewy morning had ever been spoiled by our pavements, corrugated iron and smoke, unless you chanced to know what the great mounds were which Mother Earth had now tidied and dressed with her green robes. He told of things that we often walk past without seeing, or that our work gives many of us no opportunity of ever seeing at all: he spoke of the glory of the shafts of sunlight cleaving the mist in the morning, an innocent mist that must have been very unlike our fogs, and he seemed to have noticed every one of the spiders' webs that he passed on the grass, like hammocks for a fairy queen, all shining with little jewels; and he saw lizards, which we so seldom see, running amongst the thyme. And, indeed, the whole hills seemed so new and fresh as he described them, that I hardly recognized them, and the change was more due to the freshness of his appreciation of them than to all the change the futuroscope saw that was made by five hundred years.

Thus he described the hills over which he went, and passed with his boyish tale over that horizon which bounds the view from my window, till he came to lands of which I know nothing, lands that were once ten miles from the outer edge of London and over much of which London is still to creep. But London was gone, and only wide strips of briars indicated roads that had once run towards it, now a dense home for forest badgers and rabbits, formed by both hedges flowing outwards and creeping inwards and meeting. These too he told of, and of great mounds covered by clematis and convolvulus, without the slightest idea of what they were indications, or any wish to know. Had it been possible for me to speak to them I doubt if I should have told them a single word about what could be done with the iron ore, lumps of which still lay on the hills, far less anything about steam or electricity, to bring up again over that beautiful scene the pavement and bricks of cities, and over them the fog with the factories that poison it, and their pride and power that sooner or later bring on the disaster that ends them. It was a very different world from what we know that he told of as he looked from the high ground towards Bromley and saw the plumed reeds waving by the shore of the lake, and marshes and forested islands that now filled the crater.

"Did you catch a pike?" asked his mother, not because she could not see that he had not got one, but evidently to show that she thought such an achievement was well within his power.

"No," he said. "But I saw a monster as big as Toby, and he looked at my bait and wanted to take it. But something distracted him just at the wrong moment."

And he gave a further description of the pike, which I do not repeat, because it was so greatly exaggerated, though there were in it some very vivid flashes of accurate description. Then he told of the flocks of ducks with which the lake in the crater seemed to be crowded, mallards, shovellers, widgeon, teal, sheldrake and tufted duck, which I recognized easily from his vivid descriptions, and several more which he described clearly too, and which I only failed to identify through my own ignorance. Alf said little, as the boy's delighted chatter rippled on, but I rather gathered that he might have shot a swan, had he stalked quietly through the reeds instead of giving Bill a chance to fish. And then Bert entered the hut with his story of the stag, about which Toby was the first to find out all for himself. For he ran up to welcome Bert back safe from the wood, and as soon as he had done that he began sniffing about his hands, and even his clothing, to find out just what had happened, and found to his great satisfaction that a stag had been killed, and dragged a little way and left in the wood.

"Did you get a stag?" his mother asked, though I think she knew at once from his face that he had.

"Yes," said Bert. "And it was a young one."

From the tone of his voice I could tell that he was as proud of having shot a six-pointer as one of our sportsman would have been had he killed a royal; and I realized that I was back with primal things and that our love of sport is descended from primal needs, and that in this remote past which had somehow got round into the future, tender meat came before most things.

"Where is it?" his mother asked.

"It got too late to drag it," said the boy. "So I hid it under stones and bracken, and I'll go back for it tomorrow."

"That is right," said his mother.

This was one of the many occasions on which I found it very annoying to be unable to speak along the futuroscope into the future, so that I could only get whatever information they chose to give me. But I saw that there must be some reason why it was harder to drag a stag home when it was late, so I tried to think it out, and the mother's quick agreement with the boy helped me. I took it that the danger of wolves increased in the evening and the weight of a stag would be too great a handicap if they came, and that the scent of it might even bring them. So he had buried it under stones and hidden the heap with bracken, and would bring it home by daylight. This was news, first of all the boy's safe return, and then his killing the stag, which one saw in every face, including Toby's, was something of vital concern to this people who lived among primal necessities, as no doubt we do too, but they were all bare and easy to see. No flagging interest had to be worked up artificially among these people, but all that interested them was with them already, as ready to be awaked by any one of the daily events on which their simple lives depended as was Toby out of his sleep by the howl of a wolf. All faces were bright with the good news of food; and then suddenly, as I was watching them, their expressions changed and that air of alert listening came over them all and Toby growled in a low voice. What it was that their keen ears heard I could not tell, whether it was the wild man whooping in the distance or whether they heard the sound of some distant pack hunting. For some while I watched and listened till the strained look passed from their faces and they set down to their supper again, and I began to think of mine and left them and come back home. That is to say I switched off the futuroscope and went from it into my dining room, a distance of five yards and about five hundred years.

Chapter VIII

It is not my habit to get up before eight in the morning, but I came back from that far future so much interested in the eager talk of these boys about their sport that I got up for once with the dawn and went after a very early breakfast to the futuroscope, because I felt sure that that was the time at which Bert and probably all of them would be setting out from the hut. By fumbling with the time-knob I could have got that hour at any time of day, but I found it far the best to leave the time-knob exactly where it was and let the hours pass over it at the same rate that they were passing over me; then I knew exactly where I was. I joined the instrument up to the mains, and there I was looking into the hut as the sun was peering over the eastern hill. Just as I thought, they were all up and about, and I was just in time to follow Bert from the house and up the hill, past the sheep which his father was already driving afield, and into the beechwood. He had his bow with him and a spear slung over his shoulders. The spear was of sharp flint perfectly shaped, all shining and shadowy with the little hollows from which flakes had been driven off. The arrows being in a quiver of leather, I could not see their heads, but I knew that they were of the same sharp flakes of flint which I had seen in the hut. They were fletched with grey feathers which seemed to be those of geese. The wood was dark with the huge boles of old beech-trees and the canopy of their great branches.

As I followed Bert through the wood with the luminous disk, I easily kept him in sight, but whenever I lost him behind one of those great trees I was never able to find him again by sound, for he wore the skin of some animal tied over his feet and moved noiselessly, so that I was only able to pick up the sight of him again by luck. We came, he and I, to where bracken and foxglove grew, by which I knew that we must have got above the chalk and come on the sands or gravels that lie on the top and crown our highest hills. He moved faster than I could have walked, but it amused me to chase him and overtake him with the merest touch of my finger, and to know that, for all the woodcraft the young fellow had, all the lore of the forest, he had no idea that my sight was beside him, watching every step that he took. A man with a telescope may watch another who has no idea he is watched; but who has watched another from five hundred years ago? Not many, I think, besides me; for Methery makes little use of his instrument and has shown it to very few.

We had not gone far with those long strides over the hills and my luminous circle following, when the boy came to a heap of bracken lying flat and stopped and threw it aside, disclosing a heap of large flints. And as he picked up the first flint, I saw that it rested on the body of a red deer, whose hide shone like autumn tints in the bright green of the bracken. He grallocked it, as sportsmen of our day say in the Highlands, and then cut off one of the haunches, which he left lying on the ground, and then put the rest over his shoulder and carried it back some way down the hill in the direction in which he had come. Presently he put it down and collected some more flints and covered it with them once more and hid the heap with bracken. Then he returned to the haunch and went on with it over the high ground away from his home. I could not make out at the time what he was doing, but thinking it over afterwards I saw that, if he had left the body of the stag hidden in the same place where he had grallocked it, any predatory creatures that had been attracted by the smell of the entrails, or any that saw them, would soon have come on the meat, and if he had dragged the body they would have easily followed. So he carried it to its second hiding-place and came back for the haunch. Flies began to follow us; but of course they could not trouble me, except when they got between the futuroscope and the luminous disk that it cast, when one of them would momentarily cause a little eclipse that seemed out of proportion to its size.

We came to a part of the wood where I remembered Spanish chestnuts growing, where in fact they are growing now, where the wood ends just beyond them; but it rambled on as I saw it through the futuroscope. They were saplings as I remembered them, as they are now, and used to be cut down every four years or so, I think to make palings; but here they were great trees with wrinkled trunks. Here and there we came on beeches growing among them, and bracken grew thickly, and whenever we came on a clearing it was all purple with foxgloves. And then we came to an orchard that I remembered at the edge of the wood; that is to say it grows there now; but it was all gone back to crabapples, an orchard for wilder things than men; and the forest swept on beyond it till we came to an enormous boundary of brambles and thorns, through which the boy clambered and crawled slowly by a track that he seemed to know and came upon open country the other side. And I recognized this great obstacle about fifty yards across as being the hedges of the main road from Tunbridge to London, gone wild for hundreds of years. Though we came to open land, it was entirely surrounded by forest, through glades of which I sometimes saw in the distance the flash of the water which filled so much of the great London crater. And then I saw what I so rarely saw, as I swept the light of the futuroscope over the country, another hut, its dark thatch showing up very little against the background of forest; and beside it was what we should call a kitchen garden, for potatoes were flowering there and I saw the bright flash of scarlet runners, but, without gravelled paths or box-borders or any regularity whatever, it had none of the neatness of our gardens.

And just at the edge of it under an oak-tree was sitting an elderly man dressed in deerskins. To him the young man went up and offered the haunch, which the elderly man received gratefully. I supposed that this was some kind of barter; but nothing was offered in exchange, and very soon Bert turned round and went back by the way he had come. But when we came to the orchard at the edge of the forest he sat down and waited. I say we because I accompanied him still with my luminous disk. After a while he gave a low whistle, and still he waited. And then coming along the edge of the old orchard whose huge trunks now supported only small apples I saw walking a girl with a springy tread, which in our time we associate with the hooves and paws of wild animals rather than high-heeled shoes. She walked watchfully along the edge of the wood of which it was a part, but as though knowing some dangers lurked in it. When she saw Bert her face lit up with a smile that reminded me somewhat of moonrise, and Bert rose to meet her. And now the object of that walk over the hills and the hiding of the stag killed the day before, and the gift of the haunch, became clear to me, and even the whole story of Bert's life. A proverb or saying came absurdly into my mind, a thing that could really have no bearing on this situation, "two's company and three's none," and, acting on a rather silly impulse, I withdrew my light from the pair and ran it back to the hut to see what the others were doing.

When I contracted the light and entered the hut with it, only the mother and daughter were there, and luckily I was able to pick up from their remarks the direction in which Alf and Bill had gone, which was to the lake of the crater to fish for pike again. The way they had taken was a good deal to the right of where Bert had gone, and more what we should call Londonwards. So, widening the light again, I moved it out of the hut and, running it over the hills on the western side of the Darenth, it was not long before I picked them up. Young though Bill was, the two of them moved with strides which I could never have kept up with on my feet. We went along grassy slopes on which other sheep were grazing, and saw bright patches of thyme, and sky-blue borage shining, and orchids, which were so abundant on Kentish hills when I was young and which had evidently survived the two disasters of the great explosion and the terrible snow, as well as the habits of trippers of our time, who, annoyed by their tough stalks, pulled them up by their roots; and at the top of the hills we came on foxgloves and then to the forest. It is pleasant to travel like this, sitting in a chair and seeing so much and being able to examine so much with a mere turn of one's finger, and the public should realize its advantages. Indeed it is largely to acquaint the public with these advantages that I am writing this book, and without any pretence that it can equal television in entertainment I do urge that it covers some ground which even television cannot. I know it is not on the market, but what I suggest is that, if what I write can have succeeded in awakening the interest of anyone in this instrument, he should write to the Minister for Future Affairs to ask that steps should be taken to put this useful instrument on the market.

Let me give a further description of its uses. I was using it now to follow the two boys to the lake, not so much in order to watch their fishing as to examine that very interesting formation which I have called the great London crater, and which, although it had been in existence for only very few centuries when I saw it, will almost certainly mark the earth for ever, or at any rate for as long as the craters mark the moon. And for that matter the little craters put down in Kent by the Luftwaffe during 1940 have a very enduring quality too, and I distinctly saw the marks of them after something over 500 years. Well, following the boys through the forest, we came out on the grass and thyme on the other side, but there was no grazing for sheep on this side, for the grass very soon ended where tall weeds were waving and the wide lake stretched before us, with the hills of Sydenham, lower than they had been, appearing as islands. To the boys, to whom the names of Bromley, Bickley, Beckenham, Dulwich and Kennington meant nothing, and to whom the lake had been there always, though their parents had dim legends of its coming, the scene was only a glorious home of pike and swans, and ducks of many different kinds. Both of them had bows, and Bill had his fishing-rod. Presently Alf made a sign with his hand, and Bill dropped at once and remained still, crouched under the tall reeds, and there he stayed while Alf vanished. My disk of light was wide, taking in a great part of the landscape, and in it I could not see Alf, for with the tall reeds and their plumes and the wild-rose-bushes that clothed the narrow strip of grass between the wood and the lake, concealment was easy. And it seems strange to talk of wild-rose-bushes when everything that I saw was wild and they were no wilder than any other flowers, or the orchards or swans or the men. Clematis also leaned heavily upon the branches of trees and rambled along what had been the London road and strayed out into the grassland.

More birds were on the lake than I had ever seen on water before; swans, ducks, seagulls, waterhens and birds that I did not know, and here and there I saw herons at the edge, standing in the water and fishing. I saw a swan that was some way out from the shore, and yet not in deep water, because I saw its long neck go down, and it must have been eating something that grew on the bottom. While its head was down I saw a small splash hit the water a little beyond it and then another on the shoreward side, and before its head came up I saw what it was that had made the splashes, for two arrows which had dived into the water floated up to the surface. Then the swan's stately neck came back to the bright air and I watched it gliding slowly through the lake, and suddenly its wings rose wildly and its head drooped and it was dead. Four or five other swans that were swimming near rose and flew away, making the air musical with their flight, but no other bird seemed to notice. I narrowed the light of the futuroscope and brought it full on to the swan and saw that the third arrow was stuck in its body and blood was coming from the wound and the swan's mouth. Then I examined the other two arrows floating on the water, fletched with goose-feathers and tipped with small grey heads of sharp flint, so thin that they were nearly transparent as water. Then Alf rose up from the reeds and made a sign to Bill, who rose too, and Alf went back to the grass and laid his bow down and took off the cloth cloak with which he was dressed, and removed his hide shoes and waded in to the swan. Though he had fifty yards to go he did not have to swim, and he got the swan and carried it back to the land, after picking up his two arrows that were floating upon the water. A flock of mallards that were on the water swam further away, but did not trouble to rise.

While I was watching Alf, Bill had evidently waded through the reeds till he had come to open water, and was there casting for pike. He was using something like the gaudy bait that we use for a pike, only that there was no metal in it whatever, something that seemed to be made of bone taking the place of the bright metal of the spoon-bait that we use, and a bunch of bright dyed wool was tied at the end of it, so that I saw that these people evidently had dyes. A waterhen dived not far away and did not come up again, from which I gathered that pike were plenty. While Bill cast and dragged his bait through the water I turned the futuroscope back to Alf and saw him enveloped in the brilliant light of the swan, carrying it back to the shore. There he put on his cloak of cloth again and his shoes of raw hide. Then there came a scream from Bill and a disapproving look on the face of Alf, from which I gathered that these people were chary of noise and economical with it. I turned the futuroscope back to Bill and saw him apparently repressing further yells reluctantly, for he had hooked a pike, which was pulling hard at the line and was evidently a big fish. Bill did not move back towards the shore, as, if he had done so, his line would have been entangled with weeds, but Alf came out to him with his sharp flint spear and Bill slowly gained on the pike till he had it within a few feet in the shallow water, and then Alf speared it and they got the pike to land. From the intense delight on Bill's face all this time I saw that this must be his first pike and, as I should say that it weighed from ten to twelve pounds, his rejoicing was intense.

Before I left the lake with my luminous disk I widened the disk as far as it would go, and ran it all over that glittering scene through which the lake and its islands stretched all the way to some dim hills which I could not identify, grey along the horizon. In that crater swans and ducks and all kinds of other waterfowl must have bred for hundreds of years and, as men had greatly decreased and all their deadlier weapons had gone and only the arrow come back, they must have lived with safety from everything except being stalked from cover, as Alf had stalked one of them. But their danger from man was now no greater than that from any other predatory creature, and I saw from the way that the flocks swam away from Alf and Bill when they went into the water that they accurately gauged the distance of the danger from man, as they do today and must always do in order to survive.

For long I swept the disk over that great expanse of water which lay in the London crater and over the flocks of waterfowl, and then I turned it back to see what Alf and Bill were doing, and I soon picked them up going back from the lake and on their way home. They had got to the woods before I picked them up and Bill was waist-high in bracken. Then, whether or not it was the scent of the blood of the swan that it had picked up, I heard the long howl of a wolf, which was taken up at once by two or three more. The gruesome sound chilled my blood and really did make me feel cold, though it need not have done had I thought how many centuries I was away from it. And at once the two boys began to run. So great was their speed when they ran, that they evidently relied on it and did not think of climbing a tree, and I had some difficulty in keeping them within my luminous disk, which I had narrowed down to a few paces across, until I realized the pace at which they were moving. Sometimes Alf stopped suddenly and ran back a few yards without a word or sign to Bill, as far as I could hear or see, but Bill ran back with him at once and they jumped off their trail sideways and took another line. I halted my disk at this spot to see if that dodge of theirs would throw the wolves off the scent, and very soon the great animals that they called wolves appeared, eight of them, and it did throw them off the scent for some moments, but only for very few, and they soon picked it up again and were on after the boys. They were bigger than any Alsatians that I have seen, and very like wolves, which they could not have been exactly, unless the wolves at Whipsnade had got out after the disaster to men and bred with the Alsatians. Now and then the leader gave a long howl and the others took it up; otherwise they went with as little noise through the wood as is made by wind-blown leaves. They were much faster than the two boys, but they had not gained, so far, because of the time they lost when the boys dodged, and I lifted the light off them and ran it on through the wood to see if they would dodge again; and so well had they done so that it was long before I was able to find them. When I did find them they were still running easily with apparently no fatigue, and Alf still clung to his swan and Bill to his pike. I saw Alf look at the pike and say something to Bill, but Bill only smiled and shook his head and evidently would not part from what to him was as great a treasure as any that a raider ever carried away.

And so they kept on till they came to the edge of the wood. And the wolves kept on too. At the wood's edge Alf hesitated and looked at one of the trees, for the wolves were now very close, and then he left the wood, neither getting shelter from a tree nor throwing away his swan. As he did so he and Bill turned sharply sideways and then ran on after that one more dodge. On the smooth grass of the downs and the long slope of the hill to the valley they were able to run as fast as the wolves, though the wolves had had the advantage of them in the bracken with which they were more familiar. Still, the wolves were very close, till at last the boys came to the Darenth. There they plunged in and, hiding under the left bank, they waded upstream. There I kept my luminous disk to see what the wolves would do. And the Darenth beat them. They could not see the boys, and the scent was gone with the water. Then they began to cast, as hounds do, and they did it as well as hounds with the help of the master.

Then I ran the light up the Darenth to find the boys, who had got out on the right bank and were trotting towards their home. Alf had arranged the swan more comfortably, with its head tied to a part of his clothing and its body slung over his shoulder, so that he now had both hands free to use his bow, and for the first time he had an arrow in his hand, which he had not thought of using before, as he evidently had not time for shooting in the wood or much clear view for a shot. But the wolves were now a long way away and had not yet picked up the boys' scent again. And so they reached the hut with their swan and their pike. They strolled in casually and I saw, as I turned the light into the hut when they had just closed the door and their mother and sister were admiring the swan and the pike, that being chased by wolves was an ordinary adventure, and that the thrill of it, direct though it came to them, was no more to be made a fuss about than the daily murder that is brought indirectly to us by our evening paper, and, exciting though the chase had been and the killing of the swan, I saw that the event of the day was Bill's pike.

Chapter IX

Having nothing to do that afternoon I sat for a long while over the futuroscope, keeping its disk on the inside of the hut, where the woman and her daughter were plucking the swan. They kept all the feathers carefully, though I never knew what use they had for the big wing-feathers, since I never saw any signs of writing there. But I imagine that a use was found for all material things, where they had no shops to supply them with things as they needed them, and no postal system by which to ask for the things from shops. I saw no signs of any community, for men were still very scarce, and the occupants of each hut had to supply themselves with whatever they needed. Bill and Alf seemed still to be talking about the pike. Then Bert returned, dragging the stag by its one remaining hindleg. Whether or not he had been pursued by wolves I could not tell, but I assumed not, as he could not have escaped from them dragging that heavy stag. He told his mother that he had given the other haunch to the man by the lake, as he called him; but he made no mention of the girl. Happiness and mirth prevailed in the hut that day, as ecstatically as in one of our own theatres when some merry comedy is playing, or in a pantomime. For life there depended upon daily events, as ours very rarely does, where everything is ordered and arranged for ages. If all the shops at which we get our food were to pass out of existence one day and were to reappear again several days later, we should be more easily able to understand what a successful day's hunting or fishing meant to these people of a simple age which lies in the far future. It is so that our ancestors lived long ago, and it was pleasant to me to see that our descendants, though terribly few, were still able to deal with the great problem of Earth, which is to get a livelihood from her munificence. And the more difficult and dangerous that struggle was, the heartier was the thrill when it was accomplished. There is no room for any idleness, nor any wish for it, and the thrill of sport and adventure comes nearer to them every day than it does to us through our theatres and cinemas. Perhaps in a foxhunt more than anything else we get an echo of their excitements, an echo along the ages.

Maud, the mother of the family, turned at that moment to her daughter Liza and told her to go out and pick wild strawberries; not that she called them wild, for she knew no other kind. And Liza went out with a basket of woven osiers along the grassy slopes of the valley, slopes lit with patches of thyme and strawberries and roses, much as in our time. And so they appear to me as I turn the wide light of the futuroscope on them. But I should not like to convey the impression that those slopes are exactly the same where they run down to the stream from the forest, for when I narrow the disk and look closely at them I see them all rumpled with smooth mounds which are not there when I look from my window. For between now and then a great city has stretched its streets over those downs, and, though Nature has overcome it and hidden it with her greenery, something of its outlines still disturbs the smooth faces of the hills, like a mark in a human face left by a troubled dream, soon to pass away, as the mounds of the Romans have mostly passed from Kent where they built their roads and their villas. Over these green ripples on the otherwise calm hills the girl went with her basket of osier to look for strawberries. I followed her a little way with the disk of light, and then narrowed it and brought it back to the hut, to find them all absorbed with the day's fresh supply of food. They meant to eat the fish first, and Maud had begun to cook it. How they were going to eat all the stag I did not know, for I calculated that there would be about 15 pounds of meat on it for each of them, and it was summer and it seemed hardly likely to keep until they had eaten it all, though one haunch had been given away. And after that they were going to eat the swan, but I supposed they had huge appetites. These rather greedy details were not of much interest and I was about to disconnect the futuroscope, when the door was flung open and Liza rushed in and slammed it and began running the two beams into their sockets.

"The wild man," she panted. Then I heard his bare feet outside and realized by how little the girl had escaped. The father and the two elder boys picked up their bows and threw over their shoulders the straps of the leathern quivers in which their arrows were, and pulled back the beams with which Liza had fastened the door. I turned the lighted disk outside the hut to see what would happen; but the wild man had gone as fast as he had come, and, when I picked him up, he was going fast over the slope of the downs with long strides to the south, helping his swift pace on with his two great sticks. He evidently knew, what would not take much knowing, that he had no chance against a flight of arrows by day, and though by the time that they unbarred the door he was not beyond the longest flight of an arrow, he was well beyond the range of accurate shooting. As I saw his nude figure run along the side of the hill I wondered from what forbear living now he was descended, how he is dressed today and what his habits are. Certainly none of the fashions by which we should recognize this resident in our day were in this descendant of his, and it must have been less visible things than his collar and tie that he had passed down, passions that he concealed now raging in this wild creature. The girl's father and two of her brothers waited outside the hut with their bows, till the long evening faded away and the light was too dim for shooting. Then they came back to the hut, in the doorway of which Bill had waited all the time with a spear, with the dog Toby beside him, and they slipped the beams into their two sockets and dragged up another log against the door and Liza sat still, with a frightened and wondering look on her face, and her mother was holding a spear. And now that the hut was all shut up for the night I thought of my own supper, and I disconnected the futuroscope, and the light went out and at once the hut was gone, and I saw the valley of the Darenth as it is now, before a city had come to trouble it and before disaster came to trouble the city.

Chapter X

After I had had my supper I went back for another glimpse through the futuroscope, to see that all was all right in the hut before I went to bed. They evidently went to bed early there, for I only saw the father and mother and the dog Toby now sitting before the fire, which was burning red and low. The man had an axe leaning against the wall quite near him, which gave me the idea that they might still be uneasy about the wild man who had pursued Liza. They both looked up when the dog gave the slight growl that he always gives when I turn the invisible disk of the futuroscope into the hut, but they did not know what he was growling at, nor did he.

They remained alert for some time, and then, just as all three of them were settling down to enjoy the warmth of the fire, I heard a step behind me in the night, the faint sound of a bare foot. So alarming was the sound and so close, that I spun round to look behind me, and saw the wallpaper of my own room and the frame of a picture; and of course the hut and the wild man walking round it were all gone and were five hundred years away. Still, it was quite a shock. I turned back to the eyepiece of the futuroscope, and saw his face at a window peering in; but the window was so small a space cut in the beech logs, that his face filled the whole of it and there was no possibility of his getting in by that way. None of them saw him except the dog, and perhaps he only smelt him. So softly he moved that he made no sound except the faint footfall which I had heard behind me. All the dog's hackles were up, and he rose and barked furiously and the man picked up his axe, but the face was withdrawn at once. And judging as much as anything by the dog and by the silence of the night, I gathered that the wild man had gone away. And, whether he had gone or not, I could do no good by watching. So I disconnected the futuroscope from the mains and came back down all those years and went to bed.

I was at the futuroscope next day as soon as I had finished my breakfast, and I looked into the hut, but the man and boys and the dog were all away, and Maud was at work in her kitchen and Liza was cutting some strips from the hide of the stag. And I saw once more that all the incidents of the day were to them as much the ordinary affairs of daily life as are the thrilling events of which our headlines tell, only that we are farther away from the events that thrill us, but like us they evidently looked on the affairs of the day before as news of no further interest, and went on with their shepherding, their hunting and cooking, just as we use yesterday's news to light our fires.

As there was nothing to see in the hut I switched the disk off and widened it and ran it over the hills again to look at the strange country, which I could recognize, altered though it was, till I got over the horizon that I can see today from my window and came to what no-one would recognize for the metropolitan district. And it was a lovely sight as I swept the wide disk across the crater and up and down. It was a bright summer's day, glittering on the lake, and even the reeds were shining. I turned the disk on to flock after flock of birds, the grace and brilliance of swans, the gorgeous green of the wings of teal, the darker green of the necks and heads of mallards, the flashing orange heads of the male widgeon and the delicate grey of the herons, to whom I came up quite close where they stood fishing, as I had never done before without their rising and flying away with what seemed a lazy flight, making a huge inverted W with their great wings. But now when I saw one of them in flight I found that the best of his wings was swifter than anything I could do with my two arms if I tried to imitate. And I saw water-ouzels with their black coats and white waistcoats, which dived every now and then and entirely disappeared for a while. And I saw a patch of small green leaves on the water, duckweed I believe, and to my astonishment I saw a waterhen with its red beak run across it, actually running on what I should have thought would have barely supported a bluebottle, and I saw the fantastically painted face of the water-rail; all these things probably closer than a man has ever been to wild birds before, though I was five hundred years away. And right across all this, to add a glory to what was already a glorious scene, there darted a kingfisher, a streak of the most brilliant blue Earth has to show. Waterbirds do not usually sing, but there was one song in the air all the time that I looked at the lake that had filled the crater, a song wild and beautiful that I did not know, never having heard it in London or on the dry downs of Kent, and I wondered what bird it was that could sing like that. And then it came into the sight of my disk, and I saw that it was not one bird singing but several hundred. It was a flock of golden plover that was singing, as I learned afterwards from a book, but at the time I only saw a flock sweep by at the pace of a flight of arrows, or so it seemed to me. I suppose I saw enough there, closer than others have seen, to have written a whole book on ornithology, had I the knowledge for it. But all my time has been full of wasted opportunities ever since I borrowed the futuroscope, and in the end I have only used it for my own amusement.

So, leaving the lake, I swept the disk over the grassland between it and the woods, thinking I might find Bert. For I had a shrewd idea of where he might have gone. And sure enough I soon found him. I tried the thatched cottage first where the old man was in his cabbage garden quite alone, and then, running the light along the edge of the wood, I came to the great boles of the crabapples that had once been an orchard; and there he was, sitting against one of the trunks with the girl Kate, and they were saying to each other what a fine day it was, but not in those words, for both of them seemed endowed with a transcendant perception of the beauty of all around them, so that listening to them I really learned more of what was flowering and shining all around me than I did by actually looking at it through the futuroscope. Milkwort and spurge were flowering in wide carpets at their feet with patches of thyme like rugs thrown down among them, and they spoke to each other of the sunshine, of the spurge and the heavenly blue of the milkwort, so that I saw these flowers as I had never seen them before, and they seemed to love the scent and the purple of the thyme as much as they loved each other. Something had awoken in them a wider, intenser understanding, and as I listened to them I seemed to know more of the world, more in an acre or so perhaps than I had thought there was anywhere, more beauty in each flower, more truth in the message of the songs of the birds, though I forget what that message was now. I had not got over my feeling that I was eavesdropping, which I had resisted before, but I felt unable to resist it now, as I could not have resisted peeping through the bars of the gates of Eden at Adam and Eve, had I seen them there before ever the angel came with the fiery sword. For the scene, though so far in the future, seemed, strangely enough, as fresh as the distant past, and this scene which I saw was being interpreted to me by those two; and I felt the need for interpreters, for I had lived so long in a city and been so familiar with the products of machinery amongst which we all live today, that I had somehow forgotten the ancient language of Earth which she speaks with birds and trees and winds and flowers.

They spoke of one another, but they were sitting on moss and they also spoke of that, till I saw, as though a bandage had been removed from my eyes, that it had the beauty of forests. And sometimes a butterfly came floating by, and the girl showed at once a sympathy with its grace and its brightness which somehow made me notice these things too, which I have let glide by me all my life without knowing that they were there. And on that bright morning, listening to those two as they looked at that lovely scene, the thought touched me that when I came to die I should leave a world full of treasures that I had never enjoyed. Over this coffer of jewels, this bright morning seen by two lovers, I now hung my head, conscious though I was that I was merely eavesdropping. They chattered of trivial things, and yet of what else is Earth made, unless every speck of dust which composes our planet, and every blade of grass that clothes it, are of equally profound importance.

A kingfisher flashed by again on one of his journeys, a heavenly blue streak along the edge of the lake, and turned and flashed over a wide patch of kingcups. The girl looked up and cried out at its beauty, and that much I could have done, for neither the Mediterranean nor the sky can surpass it, even though all they tell me of the Mediterranean be true, but what I could never have seen, if she had not cried out to Bert and told him, was that as the bright blue kingfisher flew low over the kingcups he astonishingly turned green. I could not believe it as the girl cried out and said so, and then I looked and saw that it was true. How this can possibly be I cannot say, but there it was. When he came to the grass again he was blue once more, and so continued as he flew on over the lake. I suppose it was an optical delusion that I saw in the futuroscope, that was also seen in the eyes of the happy girl. But I saw it. There I sat on and on watching these two lovers, when I might have made so many more useful observations, but I became enthralled by the freshness of all they said. Perhaps other lovers say the same things; but I had never been so close to two of them before while they talked to each other, and I doubt if anyone has. And the things they said, so like fantastic flights of a poet's fancy, were really there; I saw them myself as soon as they mentioned them. The boles of the ancient apple trees, for instance, which stood like druids or aged spirits guarding them, were clothed in the most delicate patterns of lichens, whose intricate beauty I saw as they pointed it out to each other, though I had never noticed it before. Perhaps I saw things once with as fresh an eye myself, but it was long ago and I had forgotten it.

They both had the light hair and blue eyes of some northern people who used long ago to raid Kent, and I was surprised to see their traces still there; yet I need not have been, for there were plenty of these children of old invaders in my time, I mean today, whose families had stayed in Kent for a thousand years already, so that there was nothing really surprising in their staying on for five or six hundred more. The girl's bright hair and her cheeks and lips were the same perfect gifts of Mother Earth as what flashed from the heads of the mallards or shone in the teal's wing, or rather I should compare them with the glow of the waterlilies, for that was the affinity that Bert found in her face, an affinity that he saw so much clearer than I, as he seemed to see all things more clearly. For he ran down to the edge of the lake where the waterlilies floated, and picked a handful and wreathed her hair with it and made a garland that he put round her neck. And her Norse beauty, that glowed as though there had never been any cities upon those downs since the old raiders had come to them healthy and vigorous from the sea, seemed to mingle with the beauty of those gleaming flowers.

I should like to be able to explain exactly how it is that the futuroscope can show us such vivid scenes; but I have never understood yet how television can pick up a sight and hurl it through hundreds of miles of air and show it as a scene at the other end. I have never understood the Heavyside layer, nor how any instrument can throw the human voice, not at the pace of sound but at the pace of light, up against it and make it bounce back again to Earth, to be heard all over it at the moment the words are uttered. Nor can I in the least understand the sound-barrier, and it is an entire mystery to me how it is that an aeroplane flying a bit faster than sound can make a bang which can break our windows. I incline to think that there is a time-barrier, through which this instrument breaks in the same mysterious way, luckily without making any of those alarming bangs, but I am not able to explain the one any more than the other. Puzzled by all of these things and delighted by all I had seen on this bright morning, I switched off the futuroscope in order to have my lunch.

Chapter XI

After my lunch I went back to the futuroscope, for really I have very little other occupation in these days. I read the papers every morning and evening, I have my meals like everybody else, I do a little tidying in this room in which the futuroscope stands, on days when the charwoman does not come from the village; and, then, I have a garden in which I sometimes work, but mostly I leave it to the flowers and vegetables to grow as they will. Certainly looking through the futuroscope has now become my principal occupation and, if some think I should make more use of it than I do in the interests of science and history, still I see no reason why I should not amuse myself with it. And so after my lunch I went back to the futuroscope, where it stands in my window, looking, as the place-knob is at present arranged, at the very scene at which my window was built to look before anything like wireless sets, television or futuroscopes were even contemplated. To be strictly accurate, the futuroscope was now looking at a scene just the other side of the hills that my window faces, but I soon brought it back to the slopes of the Darenth valley by turning the knob back to Local by a turn so slight that the eye could not have perceived it, and I soon had it looking inside the beech walls of the hut again. And there they all were except Bert, Maud and Liza, who were just finishing tidying the hut and had done it so neatly that, absurd though is the way that such thoughts arise in one's mind, I thought that my own room could do with a little tidying; and, as no-one was speaking and nothing was happening there, I came back to tidy up. When I say I came back, I rather describe what I felt. Actually, I found myself sitting in the same chair, looking out at the hills, the same chair in which, as it were, I had sailed down so many centuries. It is all rather confusing.

It was not until the twittering of some birds reminded me that evening was come, that I thought of turning my sight back to the hut. The time-knob was still so placed that the time of day, although not the time of the centuries, was almost precisely the same with me and with them. Still all but Bert were gathered in the hut, and I thought I noticed a look of anxiety on all of them, even the dog. Sometimes I thought it might have been my imagination, sometimes that it was only the alertness that those times demanded of them always, an apprehension of danger that always lurked, and sometimes I thought that it was something more than that. For a long time I watched them and only once one of them spoke, when the father said, "He should have been back by now," and I knew that he spoke of Bert. Maud nodded. Then there was silence again, a strained silence and the dog waiting and sympathising, anxious as they. And then there came the sound of a horn from over the hill and I remembered that Bert had a cow's horn slung from his shoulder, and from the direction in which the long note came I had no doubt any more than they all had that the call came from Bert, a long and wailing note sounding so mournful through the stillness of evening that I thought of the old French line:

Dieu, que le son du cor est triste au fond du bois.

And I thought too, whether foolishly or not (but one cannot direct one's fancies), of the horn of Roland at Roncesvalles. They all of them picked up weapons and went at once to the door, and the dog ran after them. But the man turned round and signed to Maud and Liza to stay behind, and told Bill to stay with them and guard them, and said much the same to the dog. So the two women stayed, and very reluctantly Bill turned back too, and even more reluctantly the dog, and the father and Alf went on up the hill to the wood, each with a bow and their quivers filled with arrows, besides which Alf had a spear and his father an axe.

With the widened light I followed them up the hill and into the wood, and on under the beech-trees in the direction of the sound of the horn. Both turned their heads all of a sudden at a sound behind them on dry leaves, and there was Toby, who had got away from the hut and followed them through the wood. Joe looked at him angrily and told him to go home, and the dog looked at him full of contrition, but would not go back. And the more he disobeyed his master's still sterner orders the more contrite he became in his head and in every limb; but, genuinely repentant though he showed himself clearly to be, he still followed. And then the horn sounded again and Joe and Alf went on and bothered no more about the dog, who came on with them. And a few short notes followed the long blast of the horn, which seemed to convey some information, though I did not know what. The two men went cautiously then and so did the dog, and I even saw by a look at Toby that he knew exactly what the trouble was. Perhaps the horn told him as it told the others, or perhaps he smelt it, for they were now not far from the horn. They were not going straight now to the place where the horn had sounded, but slanted a bit away and, when they turned from their new course, I saw that they must have been manoeuvring so as to get the wind right. And then Joe halted Alf and the dog with a sign of his hand and crept on alone, slipping through the wood and peering round every trunk, as quietly as one of the shadows of the great beech-trees leaving its tree and going to visit another. And round one of these great boles he saw what he sought, for he turned and stole back to Alf and they came on together, keeping Toby exactly behind them with signs which he obeyed.

They stopped behind the great beech trunk behind which Joe had first stopped, when, looking a little ahead of them, I saw part of a circle of wolves, sitting on their haunches, looking the other way. As it seemed a very regular circle, I estimated from the number that I could see that there were about twenty in all and, though I had not yet picked up Bert, I had no doubt whatever that this circle of wolves was waiting round him and that he must be up a tree. I do not think that Joe from where he was could see more than one wolf. He looked up at the tree behind which they both were hiding and evidently satisfied himself that he could climb it, but still seemed uncertain what to do, and I guessed from his looks at Toby that his uncertainty arose from not knowing what to do with him if he and Alf should be forced to climb the tree, and it was obvious that the two men could not take on twenty wolves on the ground. He made his son move out a little way on the other side of the tree until Alf was able to see another wolf, and then they evidently arranged to shoot together. I saw Joe draw out one of his long arrows, which seemed to be made of a reed and which was tipped with one of those sharp thin flints and fletched with what I think were a goose's feathers. He took it to his bow and drew back the cord and shot, and a howl came from the wolf, and another howl showed that Alf must have shot at the same time and hit. Then Joe and Alf ran to the tree and quickly climbed, a little way up to a low branch with their bows slung over their shoulders, and there they sat and watched, looking not towards the wolves, but to where Toby sat obediently under the tree, growling. The wolves had not seen where the arrows had come from, but they heard the men climbing the tree and the growls of the dog, and all came towards the tree and looked up and saw the two men. Two more arrows were shot at them and one hit.

Then I ran the light through the wood to find Bert, and soon saw him up in a beech-tree in the centre of what had been the circle of wolves, which had now all gone to the other tree and were jumping up at the low branch on which Joe and Alf were sitting and had not yet seen Toby, who had had the sense not to show himself round the trunk, though he still growled his threats at them. In what had been the circle of wolves I saw three lying dead, on the far side of the circle, each with an arrow in him, so that if I was accurate in my estimate of twenty there were now only fourteen. And at that moment Bert came down from his tree without going more then a pace or two away from it, and shot at any wolves he could see through the trees while they were looking in the other direction and baying at Joe and Alf. Shooting from the ground was so much more accurate than shooting when sitting up in a tree that, even though Joe and Alf were so much closer to the wolves, Bert got three more while they got one, and there were now ten and they had not yet seen Toby. I noticed that the arrows were deadlier then bullets, the long shafts that transfixed the wolves leaving them with less ability to move than bullets might have done.

And then as one of the wolves jumped up to the branch on which Joe and Alf were, although it could not reach them, Toby rushed round the tree and seized the wolf by the throat as it dropped back to earth, and the pack closed over the dog. Then Joe and Alf dropped from the tree and Bert ran forward, and for a while there was a tussle with axe and spears all in defence of Toby. In the mob of wolves and dog and men it was not easy to see what happened. I tried to keep the disk of light on Toby, but movement in that struggling heap was so rapid that I could not easily keep it on anything. But what I think happened was that the wolf that Toby pinned was the leader, and it was finished off by a spear of one of the men; and when that leader was dead the wolves all acted with less purpose, some of them snapping at Toby, some at the men, and Toby got out of the heap that had almost smothered him; and Joe and his two boys moved downhill towards their home, keeping Toby close to them, and the surviving wolves snarled behind them, but did not attack any more.

And soon they came to the sloping down on which their sheep were feeding, watched by Bill; and the wolves, which understood very thoroughly all things that concerned their lives, knew that there were not enough of them to have any chance in the open against four men armed with arrows, and the dog, and did not venture out of the wood. Joe called out to Bill, "The wolves will come no more today," and passed on without further greeting, leaving him and his sheep in the sunlight, which had not yet quite left the western hill. I followed them with the light all the way to the hut, then narrowed it and ran it inside to see their greeting after their great adventure. But they walked in casually and wiped their blood-stained spears and the axe, and merely told Maud and her daughter how many wolves they had killed. And I saw once again that their fight with the wolves was merely one of those daily struggles for life which they looked on as a part of it, and which gave life its zest. And Toby lay down by the fire and licked his wounds with an air of quiet contentment. And there I left them, disconnecting the futuroscope and going back five hundred years to have my supper.

And, when I had had my supper, the fancy took me to have one more look at them in their hut before I went to bed. So I connected the futuroscope again with the mains and, the knobs being exactly in the same places, I was back again in the hut at once. They were all sitting, rather drowsily as I thought, at their long table of beechwood at which they had finished their supper. It was by now dark outside and not very easy to see things inside, for their illumination of wicks floating in fat, which seemed perfectly satisfactory to them, seemed a very poor illumination, even when helped by the glow of the fire, to one accustomed to electric light; and, as I think I explained, the disk of the futuroscope added no light to the scene. I think the dim light and their evident drowsiness made me drowsy too, and I decided that it was time to go to bed. Nor should I have observed very accurately had I stayed at the futuroscope longer, for a sleepy man does not observe well, yet I sometimes wish I had, for just before I drowsily turned the futuroscope off I heard a hoot from the wood and recognized the wild voice of the man with the two great sticks, who always seemed to me so like the Long Man of Wilmington, and I wondered what savage impulse was moving him through the wood.

Chapter XII

And now an idea came to me that, pleasant though the futuroscope was and though I needed no other amusement with which to pass my days, yet I was not justified in spending all my time in amusing myself, when, as it suddenly had occurred to me, I should have been warning statesmen of any disasters that I might see in the future. I had not seen much as yet, and I was very reluctant to turn the knob back much earlier than where I had it, for fear of bumping again into that terrible flash which had injured my eyes already, and which I feared might even cause blindness if I unwittingly saw it again. Water from my eyes, my doctor assures me, is no longer radioactive; but it has been a warning, and I do not want to risk it again. It is a barrier that I do not like to approach, cutting me off from a certain area of the future. Still, there are plenty of spaces of time that I can cover, and I decided to search them with a view to warning our statesmen of some of the worst disasters I saw in the future. In order to do this I saw that it was necessary to learn a little more about politics than the average voter. For to speak to politicians at all I felt I must know something of their language and a little of what their speeches revealed that they were planning to do. So for some days I did a good deal of reading, not only of the political pamphlets of the party to which I belonged, but of a considerable number of reported speeches, and by the end of the week I was beginning to know a good deal about our contemporary politics, from which I got some idea of the way of politics in general.

My more serious purpose took up so much of my time that I should probably never have looked at the hut again, concentrating entirely on warning the appropriate offices of the Government of all disasters that I was able to pick up in the future, had not one thought occurred to me suddenly as a flash of lightning, after I had been at work on politics for little more than a fortnight. And this thought, surprising although it was to me, was a perfectly simple one, being no more than that, if the futuroscope was accurate, and by thoroughly dusting it and oiling the knobs I was careful to make sure that it was, then whatever it saw in the future was going to happen, and I might just as well try to alter a gramophone record by making a conductor having conducted otherwise in the past, as try to remove from the future anything that the futuroscope had seen to be there. This thought may seem obvious to my reader, and indeed it was, but I had not thought of it before, missing it as one misses many simple things; and so when it came to me it came like a shattering shock. I gave up all interest in politics at once, I gave up any hope of doing anything useful, and, with my brief ambition gone, fell back on the futuroscope as merely a very pleasant means of passing my days for as long as Methery let me have it, a harmless amusement on a par with the cinema and those other entertainments with which the marvels of our age provide amusement for other people.

So the first thing I did on giving up my brief ambition was to go to my futuroscope and, by slightly turning the place-knob, to look at the land between the old orchard and lake, where the old man's hut stood by its cabbage-garden on the slope of grass running down from the woods to the great London crater. And I had not run the disk far from the hut, when I saw Kate sitting alone. It was a lovely afternoon and the air seemed full of butterflies floating on the scent of the flowers with which the downs were so copiously brightened, marjoram, thyme, centaury and the latest of the orchids; and scabious was shining there, pale blue, tinted with mauve, with burnets sleeping upon them. Kate was all alone. I had gone there with my luminous disk because I had expected to see Bert and her, sitting on one of those slopes or in their old apple-orchard, and had thought to share their joy in the beauty of the morning, because it was so much more intense than mine is in anything now. But Bert was nowhere near. Why, I wondered? And I ran the light back over the hills to the hut. And there Bert was, sitting disconsolate. All the rest were out except his mother, and again I wished that I could have spoken, and asked what the trouble was, whether or not they would have regarded a voice from five hundred years away as having any business with their affairs. But I could not do so, and that is the principal deficiency in Methery's otherwise remarkable invention.

And so I had to judge by no more than the expression of Bert's face, as he sat there silent, and it clearly said that he had been forbidden to go where he wanted to go. And it was not long before a chance word from his mother made it all clear: his father had forbidden him to go any more over the hill in the direction in which London used to stand, for the very good reason that rescuing him from the wolves that were in the woods on the way to the crater wasted time which was very valuable. Our ideas of values are of course different from theirs, and it sounded to me, when I first heard time referred to by Bert's mother as valuable, that time spent looking after some sheep while they grazed, and making cheeses and chipping flints and cutting up timber could hardly be looked on as being of any value. But then, as I said, our values are different, and I was beginning to see that their lives depended on little daily details that we leave to our grocer, our butcher, our milkman, and others, without considering any of them of any importance whatever, and I saw that I would have to get over, if I could, the feeling that a battle of three men with a herd of wolves was scarcely a waste of time that could have been spent making cheese. So I sat looking at that disconsolate young man in the hut, while I readjusted my values.

"The wolves are not always there, Mother," said Bert. And they argued for a while. Or rather Bert argued, while his mother merely stated facts. But he was not in the mood to let facts convince him, for it was not logic that guided his arguments, but the vision, which was always dazzling his mind, of the girl on the sunny slope that went down from the wood that sheltered the descendant of one of our orchards, to the sheet of water that shone in the great London crater. I was about to turn from the profitless argument, when Bert's mother said: "And there is another reason."

"What?" asked Bert.

"The wild man come again last night," said she.

"I did not hear him," said Bert.

"We saw his tracks," she said. "You must stay here and help to protect Liza."

Her remark seemed to fall like another fetter chaining Bert to the hut, and in silence he seemed to accept it, and I wondered if the fetters would hold him. And I wondered where the wild man was, what he was doing, and what was the motive of his prowlings. So I withdrew the light from the hut and widened it and ran it up and down the country to look for him, but saw no trace of him in the woods or on all the slopes of the valley. And then, as I still searched vainly, I came to a lane, the only road I had seen as yet in this far future through which I wandered alone. And along the lane I saw coming a band of gypsies. One thing, the moment I saw them, surprised me so suddenly that I felt the surprise before I quite realized what was the cause of it, and that was that round the hub of the wheel of their cart, and on the harness of the pony that dragged it, were bits of metal, and I saw that one of the gypsies carried a knife. This surprised me immensely, for I thought I had got into a world in which metal was used no more. But I need not have been surprised, for the gypsies had never really entered our civilization, and when it was shattered it is improbable that any would have survived in the towns at all, and the gypsies in their waggons in the open would have had a better chance. And evidently now they concerned themselves with the ways of the other dwellers in Kent little more then they had with ours; and steel and iron, which were a curse to the rest, seemed not to trouble the gypsies. The advantage of steel knives is obvious, and the gypsies saw them. I am inclined to think that the others took the longer view.

So the gypsies came jingling along the lane with brass on their harness and gold ear-rings, and scarves of bright colours, looking less changed by disaster than anything else I had seen except the slopes of the downs. They seemed like observers looking at ruins of a civilization in which they had never had part. But they only seemed to look at it cursorily, as they passed through it with their carts on their very long journey, for they were travelling still. Up out of the past they seemed to come, like mourners, I thought, for our cities. And yet, would they mourn for them? Would they not rather be on the side of Nature, with her woods and her grass slopes, her streams and her flowers, which had at last regained their freedom from the domination of cities due to some weakness in the mighty force that had ruled them, as is the case with all revolutions? I moved closer so as to hear what they thought of it all, and to learn where they were going. But they were speaking a language I did not know, the old tongue of the gypsies.

Chapter XIII

All the rest of that day in my home I found myself wondering how Bert and Kate would meet, with the wolves between them, and his father refusing his help, and my curiosity was excited about the gypsies and the nocturnal roamings of the Wild Man. In fact, here was I in Kent in 1955 and not very far from London with all my thoughts and interest wandering away into the future at least five hundred years. Well, I suppose there are others who are as out-of-date, probably more than we think, only caring for some old period of history, the records of it both real and imaginary, and treasuring whatever jetsam and flotsam from it that may drift down the ages to them under the name of antiques. Had they the curious instrument that I have they would be just as likely to place their interests in the future, which was now gathering up all of mine. So I turned on the light of the futuroscope next morning and ran it over the countryside, whose features I recognized as one may recognize the outlines of the bones in a face much altered by age. Woods had increased everywhere, roads were gone, and there was still the lane I have mentioned, which I recognized as following exactly the line of the old Sevenoaks-Dartford road which crosses the Pilgrims' Way in the village of Otford, and, as I ran the light along this road, I picked up the gypsies again.

With bright scarves wound round their heads, and golden ear-rings glinting, they were very easily picked up, and they seemed to have altered less than anyone else. I saw now that they would pass near the hut of the family that I was getting to know so well, although they had never seen me, and before I had watched them strolling for very long beside their waggon, arched over with stretched skins upon high bent saplings, I saw some of them leaving the lane and slanting off to the left, evidently with the intention of going right up to the hut; and, as I followed them over the grass, my eye, which was becoming practised in observing such things, noticed that they passed over the line that was once the Maidstone branch of the Southeastern railway. To my now accustomed eye the marks of it were unmistakable. It was the straightness of it, far straighter than any lane or than any stream that ever flowed, which showed me it was a trace of the work of man, and knowing where it runs today helped me to be quite certain.

Soon after they crossed this they come up to the hut, and there was Bert, still disconsolate, and his mother at work on making another dish; not what we should call making another dish, meaning cooking one, but making the dish itself out of brown clay which she must have got from the top of the hill. She was smoothing it with the palm of her hand, and was evidently about to begin the long process of drying it before baking it in the fire, for she had a large fire burning though it was a warm day. And then Toby growled, and the gypsies were by the door, two men and a woman with their brown faces lit by their golden ear-rings. The door was still shut, but a gypsy man drew a piece of reed from his pocket and played but a single bar and the door was opened slowly by Maud. But the moment the door was wide enough for her, Liza ran out, for she evidently knew by the tune that it was the gypsies; and Maud and Bert followed and then Bill, and saw the gypsies standing there. And the one who had played on the pipe drew it out again and played a longer tune, standing there with a bright red scarf round his dark hair. And I could see from their eagerness that the woman knew that strange wares were to be had. And the gypsy woman with a face like that of an old brown eagle drew out from a bag she carried small ornaments made of horn are bone and ivory and tin. From the sight of the ones of tin Maud drew back suddenly, and even Liza turned away, though with less horror. And the old gypsy woman, seeing that the Englishwoman evidently feared some curse concealed in the metal, withdrew the objects of tin into her bag, and persisted in making the bone ones and the ivory ornaments carved from the tusks of boars glitter in sunlight close to the English faces. And the gypsy man with the reed pipe played on behind the old woman until she had persuaded Maud to buy a white comb of bone at the price of half a pound of cheese, and for another half pound of cheese she sold to Liza a brooch of glittering crystals hewed from a flint and set in a bright circle of greenish glaze that the gypsies had somehow run over baked pottery.

As I watched the old woman bargaining and the gypsy man playing his weird tune I could see the lure of their dark faces and bright ornaments and cunning words gripping all there; but Toby, who well knew that here was something exotic, showed that knowledge by little low growls, which persisted even though Bill had checked him more than once. And suddenly Bert asked them where they were going, and the two men both began explaining at once and pointing. They were speaking English now, as they explained their journey. They would go on up the lane still northward for a little further, the way that the Darenth was flowing; soon they would cross the stream and go up the hill and cross it wide to the right of the way by which Bert had gone when he went to the old apple-orchard and came back followed by wolves. Somewhere on that hill they would camp on a slope below the woods, through which they would go by the light of the next morning, and so come to the lake that lay in the crater, and fish there and move on and barter their fish. "I will go with them," Bert suddenly said to his mother.

"No," she exclaimed. "Your father said no."

"The wolves do not trouble them," said Bert.

And this there was no denying, for they had started on their long journey when wolves were yet in England, and were travelling still while this new breed of them were hunting in English woods.

"But you might meet them coming back," said his mother.

And that was to look beyond the vision of a young man in love, which Bert refused to do.

"I shall not take the horn," he said.

And by this he meant that he would give no more trouble to any of them to rescue him from any wolves. And when she tried to insist on his taking the horn, he said he might not return at all, but might stay over there by the lake for the rest of his life. One more effort she made to hold him. "They will bring you to their fires," she said, "and their accursed places." But he paid no heed. I think she was speaking of the forges that they must have had somewhere in order to smelt the bits of metal they had. And Maud felt that tinkering with metal and changing its shape by fire was what had ruined so much of the world, and was trying to keep Bert away from any contact with it, as though she were holding him back from sacrilege. And when she saw that he was in a mood that she could not control she said no more, and he turned to the gypsies and asked their leave to accompany them. And the two men smiled their strange foreign smile and said something to each other in their own language and the old woman nodded her head, and Bert took his spear and his bow and quiver at once, and a cheese which he gave to the gypsies; and away the four of them went to the lane to follow the caravan. Bill ran after them for a little way, enormously attracted by their bright scarves and by all that was exotic about them, and after him came Liza. And one of the gypsy men walked slower when he saw that she was following, so that she soon caught up and they walked together.

Then the old woman drew out from her bright cloak a crystal ball, perfectly round, such as must have been carved by instruments of ours and had been treasured among the gypsies all that time, since before whatever had fallen to make the great London crater, to which they were now going to fish. And she began looking thoughtfully into it, and Bill ran up to ask her what she saw; and she looked at his eyes and then at the crystal and said that she could see water in it, and him standing beside the water and a great fish coming towards him. And then she saw the fish lashing the grass and the thyme. And Bill was very happy. Then Liza came up to where Bill and the old woman were standing, and wanted to know what more there was in the crystal, and the gypsy man stood near her, listening. But there was nothing for him there. And all the old woman would say of what she saw in the crystal was: "You have wild dreams."

Joe was out on the hill watching the sheep, and I did not see Alf. Liza and Bill walked back to the hut, and the bright patch of the three gypsies faded away, till they came to the caravan and merged with the rest, an old civilization that had never strayed far from Nature, and which was surviving still among wild and natural things. And when the gypsy who had walked with Liza saw her turn back, and saw his old gypsy aunt put back the crystal under her cloak, he drew out his reed pipe and played a tune on it that might have been a farewell, were it not for merry skirls that rose in it again and again, each one of them seeming to bring to him out of the future a different consolation for what was lost in the past. And so the tune wailed and chuckled as the gypsies wandered away, until lost in the sounds and the silence that haunted the grey of the hills.

Chapter XIV

As the gypsy caravan with its one flute faded away out of sight and hearing I switched the futuroscope off, as I had a lot of small things to attend to, of no interest to my readers, but necessary if my house is to be kept tidy. One more glance I took that evening, to see if Bert and the gypsies were going over the hill to the great London crater. I ran the light over the valley after sunset and, when I saw two or three lights blinking out on the western hills just under the wood, I had no doubt that it was their campfires. They would go through the wood by daylight, and before that morning was over they would come in sight of the lake. And so I switched off for the night.

Next morning as soon as I had finished my breakfast I switched on the light with the place-knob just where I had left it the night before, and there were three grey circles of ash on the grass outside the edge of the wood, with no smoke coming from any of them, and I saw that the gypsies must have been gone some time. I ran the luminous disk through the wood, which is not very wide there, and just at the far edge of it were the gypsies, with the waters of the great crater shining before them. We must have arrived there very nearly together. And Bert was with them still, and they were all going down to the edge of the water, about a dozen of them; but well before they reached it Bert slanted away to his left, and so came soon in sight of the hut and its cabbage-garden. And suddenly I saw him look up so gladly, that I knew he had seen Kate. And then I saw her carrying a bucket of goat-skin, which she must have got from a spring, for she was some way from the lake. I found where she got the water from later, as I ran the light over the grass; it was a barrel sunk into a hole over which a small stream ran. She looked up and saw Bert, and soon they were together. Again the feeling came over me that I was eavesdropping, and this time it guided me.

Away by the edge of the lake the gypsies were singing and shouting, and I moved the luminous disk over to them. And there for some while I held it, fascinated by the lovely scene, for the sunlight was glowing and flashing all over the great London crater, and the foreground was brightened with the dyed cloaks of the gypsies and their bright scarves and trinkets, and birds that they had disturbed were wheeling over the water, and circling lower and lower as they searched the reeds to make sure that nothing lurked there that threatened danger to them. And close to the gypsies, but just out of shot of an arrow, the range of which they seemed able to calculate, floated other flocks of ducks, and some swans were adding a beauty to the lake and even a brilliance to the sunlight. All the gypsy children began to fish, and some of the men waded out to cast their lines from long hazel rods with large bright bait which were evidently for pike. Again I heard the golden plover sweep by, singing their communal song, which I heard before I saw them. And then the gypsy whose eyes had so earnestly looked at Liza drew out his pipe again and began to play strange wild notes, such as Pan might have played for shepherdesses, and he walked away in the direction in which Bert had gone, still playing his pipe. I left the gypsies then, with their pony turned loose to graze, and some of their children gathering sticks at the edge of the wood for their women to light fires beside their waggon, and the men standing dark by the edge of that flashing water, and I turned the light on to the gypsy playing the pipe and kept it moving with him. And presently he did what I had refrained from doing, and came right up to Bert and Kate, where they sat amongst the thyme, and stopped there and played his tune right in front of them. Bert looked up sharply.

"What do you want?" he asked.

"I am not playing the tune to you," said the gypsy.

Kate looked at him, strange and new to her, playing his tune, that neither bird nor man had brought to her ears before. She did not wish to speak to him, yet there was a novelty and a romance about the gypsy that attracted her eyes. Bert rose and walked up to him and the two men stood facing each other, Bert holding his spear. "Put down your spear," said the gypsy. Bert pointed to the steel knife that the gypsy wore in his belt, an old weapon that had come down to him through the centuries, as swords of Toledo have come down to us, for in this world of theirs there were no longer any furnaces that could make anything like that.

"Put down that accursed thing," said Bert.

And the gypsy threw down his knife, and I saw from Bert's glance at it as it shone on the grass that it really was to him a thing of evil that was utterly accursed for some harm it had done, or a disaster that it had led to. Kate never spoke or moved. The gypsy put his pipe back amongst his clothing, and I stepped out of the way to give them room. How silly my act was I realized immediately, but it was quite involuntary. Of course that far distant day faded at once, and I nearly upset my chair. When I got back again the men were already at grips, and the girl was watching intently. They wrestled awhile with very little movement; and then Bert was thrown over his rival's head by some trick of the gypsies of which I knew no more than Bert. He landed flat on his back and was up at once, and the gypsy was standing with bent knees, waiting to clutch him. But Bert ran at him, a far heavier man than the little gypsy, and hit him once with his fist and the gypsy went down. And Bert stood over him and held out his hand, saying "Enough, Lee." And I learned from that the gypsy's name. But he did not take Bert's hand, moving over the grass instead, without quite getting up, to where his knife was lying. For a moment Bert stood still. Then he ran back to pick up his spear, which he reached just after Lee had gripped his knife. And the two men stood facing each other again, with weapons out of two different ages, and still Kate said never a word. The spear was as sharp as the knife, but it also had length and weight, and the gypsy came no nearer.

Then Bert took another step back to where his bow lay, and very slowly lowered himself on his right knee and picked up the bow with his left hand, then put it down again and took a flint-tipped arrow out of its quiver, watching Lee all the time and still gripping his spear in his right hand. For some while he remained like that, then suddenly dropped his spear and picked up the bow and the arrow, probably while Lee's glance had turned away for an instant, for the gypsy came no nearer during the moment before Bert had the arrow strung. I wondered what Lee would do. But quicker than I could wonder he sheathed his knife and, while Bert watched him intently, drew out his pipe of reed, on which he began to play the merriest tune, and then began to dance to it very lightly upon his toes. Bert drew the arrow to its head right before him, and at that Lee smiled and went on with his tune and his dance and lightly danced away. So ended rather curiously a fight that had seemed a fight to the death and, laughter being infectious at any time and more so when travelling along bars of music, Bert also smiled. And another romance was ended for the gypsy as quickly as it was begun. But what of that? Life for him was made of romances and there would be more for so long as the sun shone and so long as he could play on his pipe of reed strange and alluring tunes. To the echoes of that tune that he was playing now as he danced away, Bert and Kate danced together on grass and patches of thyme.

I left them dancing together and followed Lee back to his tribe. There he arrived by the water still playing upon his pipe, showing no sign of defeat or a lost romance, but rather with the air of one for whom the future was full of so many romances that he only had to choose from it those that would suit him. His gold ear-rings shone in the sun. As he came down to the reedy edge of the water he came home, for the unending road was always the home of the gypsies; not that they had come through the forest by anything that we should recognize by the name of road. It had no hard surface whatever and was merely a track over sand, winding through trunks of old beech-trees where the sand lay golden on the top of the chalk and where wheels wore the track a little deeper whenever they came, which was rarely. Indeed, only the gypsies went that way, for I saw no wheels in use among any others, and it struck me as curious that they whose civilization had hardly competed with ours should in these days into which my futuroscope looked be somewhere at the edge of the iron age, while all the rest that I saw were back in the stone age. And I rather mournfully reflected that, had we been content with our iron age, we might all have remained in it, and that when the atomic age flung us out as presumptuous intruders that had no business there, we missed our iron age altogether, and were hurled right back to an age that had been good enough for our forbears.

But these reflections of mine can have no interest in a collection of notes merely designed to describe the pleasures to be found in idle moments spent at this curious machine, and I will therefore continue to jot down just what I saw, these glimpses that I have been able to have of the road ahead along which our race is travelling the years. To turn back again to the neolithic age from those gypsies with their flashes of gold and bits of iron, and steel knives treasured from our day, Bert and Kate were alone on the slope rising up from the lake to the wood.

There they sat planning their future as they looked away towards the waters of London, a future to be in a hut that Bert was to build somewhere along that slope between the forest and crater. And, as they planned, the evening wore away, and presently there rose up over the wood behind them all golden a full moon. It was not a full moon with me. Indeed as I look from my window a moon only a few days old is sinking its horns over the hill upon the far slope of which beyond my horizon Bert and Kate were sitting, I mean will be sitting under a full moon some five or six hundred years hence. I find it sometimes very confusing. I looked at that huge old moon marred by craters while they looked at its golden light in the waters below them; and I wondered if some intelligent race had lived long ago in the moon, and if by some mistake such as we had unluckily made they had made the same mess of the moon we seemed to have made of the earth.

Chapter XV

From that happy scene in the moonlight, which I will long remember, I switched off the luminous disk and disconnected the futuroscope and went to bed. I had intended often to turn the light on that hill and to watch those two sitting among the thyme and marjoram, and for this purpose I kept the place-knob exactly there, for I had felt sure that Bert would stay over there on that side of the hill, where the old man with whom he had already ingratiated himself lazily tended his cabbage-garden; and then, whatever system of marriage they had in that wild future, I was sure that Kate and he would soon be wed, and I pictured Bert building for them a rude hut. And indeed to see whether he had begun his building, more than to listen to their happy talk, I ran the light over that slope the very next evening. All over the slope I ran it and into the wood and all through the aged orchard that had gone back to crabapples and along the edge of the lake, but the only human being that I could see was the old man sitting in the door of his hut, looking up quickly at every sound of the wind or a passing bird, and always forlornly. Kate had gone. There was no sign of the gypsies anywhere by the lake; Bert was not there; only the disconsolate old man. I ran the light back to the hut in the Darenth valley, and there was Bert with all the family, and I saw at a glance that he did not know that Kate was gone. I had no possible way of telling him; I could only wait. And it was no use waiting there, so I came home again, a phrase I continually find myself tempted to use, though all I actually did was to disconnect the futuroscope from the mains, and there I was sitting at my futuroscope in the window, with only one hill between me and the crabapple orchard, and five hundred years. I had to leave Bert to find out what had happened, and I was sure he soon would.

That evening when I put in the plug that connected the futuroscope with the mains I did not look at Bert's home, but switched the light on to the slope where he used to sit with Kate, being sure he would soon come there. As he had not yet come, I narrowed the luminous disk and ran it inside the old man's little hut on the off chance of finding Kate there, but a single sweep of the light showed there was no sign of her, nor was she anywhere on the slope between the wood and the lake. The moon rose later that evening and it was not till it was flashing in the water of the great London crater from over the tops of the trees, that Bert emerged from the wood. He seemed to see at once that Kate had gone. He must have come through the old orchard and seen that she was not there, and now in the gloaming lit by that golden moon, he could see at a glance his loss. He looked all round him wondering, clearly knowing no more than I where Kate had gone. And then I think he suddenly guessed. For he looked to the reeds of the lake where the gypsies had been, and then ran down to the hut and spoke to the girl's father. But he could tell him nothing. All I heard him say was that the flute had been playing after Bert had gone, and Kate had seen him off as he went back through the wood the morning before, and he had not seen her again and the flute had gone on playing.

In what direction had he heard the tune, I heard Bert ask? And the old man pointed. And Bert turned round from him and set off at once. I should have liked to help, but I could do nothing. To begin with I should have liked to question the old man, from whom I felt sure that some clue could have been got. And then I felt I could easily track the gypsies. But what could I do if I did? I could tell Bert nothing. But, useless though it was, I determined to find out what had happened. And then I did a curious thing, at least it will seem curious to those who have never used a futuroscope, and I suppose that that is pretty well everybody: I moved the time-knob back to the day before, keeping the place-knob on the grassy slope that ran from the orchard down to the edge of the great London crater; and, no sooner had I got it back to the morning, when I saw Lee a hundred yards or so away from the hut playing his pipe of reed. He was between the hut and the reeds where the gypsies were fishing and where the cart still stood with its high roof of skins. It was certainly a strange tune, and Kate was listening, and he played it very low. Kate seemed to be interested in the tune, interested as a child would be in the song of a new bird, and Lee seemed to know when that interest was awakened. And then he moved a little further away, and went on softly playing the strange tune. And Kate walked a little nearer, though no nearer to Lee than what she had been before he moved. Soon Lee moved again, and Kate followed the tune.

Lee said no word to her and she seemed to take no notice of Lee, only of that strange tune that he was playing. After this second move I could see, as I followed Lee, the rest of the gypsies by their caravan at the edge of the water.

And then I saw some of the gypsy women, seemingly led by the old woman whom I had seen before, stroll up the hill from the water; then along the edge of the wood they moved to their right. And all the while Lee went on playing. Then the gypsy women moved down the hill, and this brought them behind Kate. Then Lee rose up and, playing the strange tune still, he stepped to where the other gypsies were fishing. As they saw him coming, the gypsies came up from the water and the women closed in behind Kate as she stood listening, though going no nearer to Lee. The pony was already harnessed; for a moment there was a scuffle; then Kate and the gypsy women reached the caravan, Kate being shown bright scarves and soothed with false explanations, and in a few more moments they were all in the cart underneath its bulging high hood. I could not say a word. It was strangely exasperating to be so close and to see so clearly an act like this, without being able to utter a word of protest, without being able to call to the girl's father to tell him what was happening or to send a word of warning to Bert. It was all over in a few moments, and the caravan was moving away with all the gypsies.

I watched to see in what direction they went, and following them was easy. There were few tracks in this land where Nature rioted with her roses, and one of those they took, one they had travelled before, for wheel-tracks were there which were very like to theirs. They were moving away in the direction of Farnborough, whose high ground stood a promontory overlooking the lake, the hooded cart in front and the men walking. All the way on their left they had the great water with its swans and great flocks of birds, and their track wound over the grass between privet and briar-roses, till they came to forest again and their sandy track wound in and out among the boles of great beech-trees. I ran the light along the track ahead of them and saw no other track by which they could go, and I noted the deep rut that their wheels cut in the sand and knew I could pick them up any time. Was ever a detective better able to follow a crime, and able to do less when he came up with the criminal? I wanted to run the light back to the hut by the Darenth and look in the face of Bert and tell him where Kate had gone, and I wanted to warn the old man. But I could do nothing.

I turned on now to the following evening, whence I had just turned back, and there was Bert disconsolate in the moonlight and I unable to help him. Then suddenly I saw that he did not need my help, for he turned quickly from the old man and went down to the edge of the crater just where the gypsies had been fishing and very soon picked up the track of the wheels, perhaps the only wheels in that part of the country, and soon was following them even in the dim light. And to my delight I saw that he was going the right way. His suspicion of Lee and the wheel-tracks deep in the sand were evidently clear guides. He was moving swiftly, rather as wolves might move, and I felt that, though he was only one to about twenty-five of the gypsies, I should not like to be followed like that. I moved the disk forward no more to see where the gypsies were, being satisfied from his very attitude and his speed that Bert would find them as surely as my luminous disk could do. But, having had two days' start, I knew they could hardly be overtaken that night, and, as it was long past time for my own supper, I disconnected the futuroscope for the night, deciding to pick up Bert early next morning when he and I would have the light of day for our tracking.

Chapter XVI

Next morning as soon as I had finished my breakfast I dashed off to find Kate, without ever pausing to think how useless it would be if I did. I had not turned the place-knob far, when I met Bert following, as I expected to find him, along the track of the caravan, an easy track to follow. So easy was it that I ran on ahead of him with my luminous disk to see how far the gypsies had gone; and a few miles ahead of Bert, going up to Farnborough I found them. Lee walked in front, still haunting the air with that strange tune of his, then came the hooded cart with the old woman driving, and the rest of the merry company straggled behind. They were still going through forest, the sandy track winding in and out among gripping roots of the trees. And then I saw them come to another track, that slanted away to the left. There were tracks of wheels there too, but older ones, not anything that I thought Bert could mistake when he came to that other track. Then I narrowed the light and ran it inside the bulging hood of the gypsies' cart. And there was Kate with the gypsy women, not bound in any way, and they were explaining to her, ceaselessly explaining, that this was the way of the world: Lee wanted her, he would look after her, he would give her all she wanted, they had all been taken away like this. There was nothing to complain about. They did not complain; why should she?

Kate would not speak. It was the way of the world, said the gypsy women again. It was foolish to complain of what all others accepted. But still Kate would not speak. And now the caravan had stopped and men were talking outside the hooded cart, and I ran the light outside and widened it to see what they were doing. They had taken the righthand track and were two or three hundred yards along from where it forked, when I turned the light to it again from inside the cart where the women were watching Kate, and all the gypsy men were bending over the track, some of them as far back as the fork. I thought at first that they were gathering something, but could not see what. And then I saw. They were smoothing over not only the tracks of their cart, but every hoof-mark that their pony had made, and even tracks of their dogs, a few of which had followed them all the way: every now and then a gypsy would discover another of those little paw-marks and smooth it over with his hand or a twig. The dogs themselves were lying down by the cart. As the men went back to the cart, having smoothed over all the tracks, they brushed over every one of their own foot-marks, where they showed at all, with a long twig behind them. I saw their trick, but it was more thorough even than that, for Lee and one or two others had gone back to the other track and were stooping over it. I turned the light full on them to see what they were doing and I saw that they were making artificial wheel-tracks, cutting them in the sand, and not only that, but one of them had two artificial hooves in his hand carved of wood, which must have been carefully carved long ago, in readiness for such tricks. Indeed this track that forked to the left was all full of tricks, for presently two gypsies walked along it with two dogs running behind them, and I followed them for some way, when each of them lifted up a dog in his arms and turned round and carried it back, stepping on hard bits of ground where they were not likely to leave their own tracks. They knew, as I knew, that Bert would follow them. But when he came to this other track in the forest would he be able to cope with the cunning of the gypsies and this elaborate trap? On and on they worked down the pathway, making the false track wherever they came to soft earth, and making the false hoof-marks all the way till they came to the lower ground and the edge of the crater again; and there they ran their tracks into the water, breaking a few reeds here and there as though the gypsies had driven their cart through the shallows. A few rags and skins and cinders they left on the water; then they came back through the forest, smoothing over their own returning tracks where any were visible. As I followed them back I met the others, still playing their tricks, and one of them was carrying fresh horse-dung along the lefthand track and I saw more scraps such as one sees by gypsy encampments, and, as I saw then, scattered along the track.

I ran the light back to Bert to see what he was doing. But there was no use in that. What I really wanted to do was to warn him, to tell him about the trap that the gypsies had laid for him, but I could not do that. And never have I felt so helpless as I did then. He was following with his spear and his bow along the way they had taken, but he was five hundred years away from me and I could not say a word to him. I was so close; I could look into his face; but I could not speak. What could I do? I felt it an agony to be so helpless. All I could do was to go back to where the tracks forked and wait. But there was no use in that. If Bert took the wrong road and the trick succeeded, I could not utter a hint. There was my luminous disk right in front of Bert, but to him completely invisible. He was following fast and I had not long to wait in the forest at the fork of the roads after the gypsies had tidied up the last of their tracks and gone on with their cart before I saw Bert approaching. I turned the light full on his face, but could not make him blink. I yearned to speak to him, but over that waste of centuries I could not send even a whisper. It was a bright sunny morning and I could see him so clearly: never have I felt so helpless except in dreams. In dreams one may sometimes stretch out a hand to touch something that cannot be reached; in waking hours it was like trying to take hold of the moon. Perhaps some child has sometimes tried to take that golden disk out of the sky, and its efforts to grip the moon were no more helpless than mine.

And then Bert came to the fork and went down the wrong way. Down that false track he went and I could not stop him. The gypsies were only a mile away to his right, going up to Farnborough, and he was slanting away towards the crater. How could I stop him? How could I speak to him across five hundred years? And just as I saw that the problem was insoluble, just as I realized that my questions could have no answer, a thought suddenly struck me. I remembered Toby. There was, then, a link between my time and theirs; a gossamer one, but a link. Though no sound could come from me along all those centuries, though my luminous disk was invisible, Toby had growled. Some influence, whatever it was, some inspiration that could not touch men or women, had been felt by the dog. How he felt it I could not guess. But he had growled. Would the gypsies' dogs feel this influence? Could I stir one of them to utter a sound that Bert could hear?

Bert was going further and further down the wrong track. I ran the light after the gypsies and caught them up with a twist of my finger and thumb, and there were the dogs trotting along behind the hooded cart in which I knew Kate was a prisoner. They were tall white dogs with tails like plumed sabres, and patches of grey on their backs, more like overgrown fox-terriers than any other breed that I know. I picked the most intelligent, as he appeared to me, and concentrated the light to as narrow a disk as possible and turned it full on him and kept it on. To my delight I saw him shake his head, as though trying to shake off a fly. But he uttered no sound. Still I kept the disk full on him. Then he shook his head again. After a while he sat down and opened his mouth. I thought he was going to howl, but he did not. I knew that Bert was slanting further and further away, and would soon be out of hearing. I clutched the place-knob frantically, keeping the luminous disk exactly on the dog, and never let him get out of it. Again he sat down. This time he scratched. So that was all I could do, and my helplessness infuriated me. Yet I was affecting the dog somehow, for he was obviously ill-at-ease; and still I kept the disk on him. He got up and trotted on, and I feared that the influence was waning, and he no longer even shook his head. And yet it was an influence: could it be cumulative, I wondered? That was my only hope, but he trotted steadily on, heedless of me. And what else could I expect from five hundred years away?

One of the gypsies called to him and he looked up; but he wouldn't look up for me. I could only cling to the place-knob and keep the disk full on him. How clear he was to me, his damp nose, his flapping ears, the curve of his tail and the bright sand that he trod on; but I could say nothing to him. And yet all the while there was this faint influence that he felt, something in the air that the other dogs could not scent or see, and of which he was dimly aware: still I held on to the knob; it was all I could do. And, just as my hope dwindled, the dog sat down and howled. It was a long quavering howl, aimed up to the sky, wailing all over the promontory of Farnborough and down to the shore of the great London crater. So I had done it. It wasn't much to have done, to make one dog howl. Others have affected the future more than that, and more than they ever have guessed, by some trivial act, but none of them had affected it quite like this, and I felt a certain glow, not of pride of course: that would be quite unjustified; but it was something to know that I had helped Bert from all that distance away, and I was sure that he would hear the howl of the dog. Lee shouted to the dog to keep quiet, and Bert may have heard the shout too. I ran the disk at once through the forest away to the left till I brought it on to the other track, and there I soon picked up Bert. He was standing quite still and listening.

A dog barking with us may mean anything, but there where men were so few it almost certainly meant that the gypsies were passing, and that either one of their dogs was giving tongue, or that their wild retinue had awakened the just suspicions of some dog guarding the hut. I waited long to see what Bert would do. I could do no more for him. Still he listened, but when no more sound was heard from the gypsies he looked again at the track, the false one that they had made. It was certainly well laid out, and for long he hesitated between the obvious track and the far howl of the dog. Then something he saw on the track seemed suddenly to wake his suspicion, and he turned to his right at once and went with his spear through the wood.

Chapter XVII

That single howl of the gypsies' dog was all I could do for Bert and the girl he had lost. It is a small effect to have had on the future, but all I could do for them. The gypsies travelled far from the spot where the dog had howled. Having concealed their tracks for nearly a mile, they were contented with their ruse and no longer troubled to cover them any more, and moved the quicker for that. Kate had never spoken to the gypsy women who guarded her, and sat immersed in her melancholy. But when the dog howled she looked up alertly, with a gleam of hope in her face, which Mrs. Smith saw at once. Mrs. Smith was the sly old woman who had told Liza's fortune back in the Darenth valley, and who had been driving the cart; but she was inside the cart now, watching Kate, and she told the others to put a light gag over Kate's mouth, which they did with a bright scarf. Kate saw from this that the gypsies thought, what her own heart had told her, that Bert was not far away, and she hoped that the dog would howl once more, and she prayed that it would to whatever dark gods of the forest she worshipped; but the dog made no more sound and she feared they were far away, hunting. Again the gypsy women said it was the way of the world, and told her to be cheerful, and Kate would not reply. Then the hill steepened and they all got down from the cart, and some of the gypsy men pushed it. The scarf was still over Kate's lips, and nobody made any comment. Now they came to great oaks, with mistletoe growing on some of them, at which the gypsies gave glances which seemed to me reverent, as though in this far future time, with cities and civilization gone, the mystery of mistletoe had come into its own again.

From Farnborough and what we call Hayes Common they saw through glades in the forest the heights of Sydenham, and the waters of the great crater flashing below them to their left. After Bromley the land dipped, and their track wound wide to the right to avoid the water which lay deep over what we call Downham, and only a narrow strip of forest joined the dry ground with Sydenham. Before they came to this eminence that looks on the great London crater they ceased their slow walk, for the pony could not pull their cart at much over two miles an hour along that rough track, even when the women all walked, as they usually did, and when all the gypsies sang to the tune of the reed pipes to help them all along. But now they were silent, for some instinct they all had told them that they were followed. Even the children were silent, dark wild creatures who ran about all over the track and in and out of the forest. I do not think they knew much about Kate or had any fear of pursuit, but the moment the silence fell they felt at once some uneasiness troubling the caravan and hushed their own wild voices. Half way up that promontory that rose from the water, now all alight with the glow of the setting sun, the gypsies halted and made their camp for the night. Tentpoles they never carried, for they were a forest people and supports for the hides that sheltered them grew in abundance all along their endless journey. The women had taken the gag from Kate's lips, but two of them sat very close to her, one on each side ready to gag her again should she attempt to call. Then they lit fires for cooking, and the sight of them cheered Kate. But Mrs. Smith saw the light of hope in her face and said to her, "Our tracks are well covered."

Evidently the gypsies trusted to that, or knew that, if they were followed, their tracks for the last few miles which they had not covered would be sufficient guide to whomever pursued them, so that their fires would make no difference; but they kept them low for all that. The great boles of the beeches which had been lonely all day, and perhaps for ages, were a citadel now of the gypsies. The mosses of their great surfaces shone in the firelight, and beyond the shining trunks unlit ones made a great darkness. And just at the edge of that darkness Kate saw the black bulk of a hut, with a red fire suddenly gleaming out from the dark of it. She watched it only, I thought, because it caught her eye, then saw that the glow increased more quickly than any fire she had seen, as it rose and fell like some fiery spirit panting. And then she saw to her horror that it was no natural fire, but something the gypsies fanned with what we know to be bellows, and she knew that she looked on one of those things of which she had heard from her father, a thing accursed and never to be approached, the ancient source of disaster, a forge that melted metal which once had ruined the world. Horror and sacrilege seemed blended in that fire, and added to Kate's misery.

I do not think that I can have been mistaken in what I saw in her face; it was all so clearly written there while I watched her. We who are so much more sophisticated cannot easily imagine horror felt at the sight of a forge. But Kate felt nothing less, as I could easily see, and evidently she had seen what it was before I did, a very crude little forge. To imagine her feelings, which I saw so clear in her face and in her shrinking movement away from it, we should picture someone making a hydrogen bomb before our eyes in a spirit of mere mischief. As we should look if we saw such a thing, so Kate looked now as she saw the glow of that little fire, so far as I was able to see, and something more than that, for it is only one reason that would turn us away from such a sight as that, but Kate's expression of horror seemed to come from something deeper, and I remembered the scene in the hut by the Darenth when the boy brought in the old axe-head, that thing that she saw was sacrilege, something condemned by the wisdom of the ages. We fear that harm may come from the interference of Man with the atom; but they knew. This simple people had a lore that the ages distilled, they did not know how, they only knew that a warning had come down the centuries, and the warning told them to keep away from those first steps which led to the steam-engine, and then to the use of petrol and so to disaster. So with horror all over her face, as though she saw coming near what could not really return for many centuries, Kate seemed glad to turn from what was so dreadful to her, when the women led her away to a little fire of their own.

Then I touched the knob of the futuroscope, the merest touch that made the light quiver forward a few yards into the hut that had so horrified Kate, and there I looked round to see what it was all about. It was a tiny hut, a mere shelter to keep the rain off the forge, and a gypsy there was working a pair of bellows on a fire that was only of timber, to make a small piece of iron red hot. What he wanted to shape it to I could not see. The thing itself was only some long, rusty nail that he had probably got out of a railway sleeper, or the decomposed remains of one. By the small fire to which they brought her the women sat down and began to cook venison, tender pieces of which they offered her as soon as they were cooked, telling her to make a good meal; but she must have been still too horrified by what she had seen, for she would not eat anything. The men kept to their part of the forest, some twenty yards away; the small fires sank to red embers, the stars shone more brightly where they peered through the great branches, the gypsy children were all asleep, the women that watched had finished eating the venison, and then into the trunk of the oak under which they sat there silently slid an arrow. They all looked up and another went into the oak just beside it and then a third, three arrows in a neat row. The arrows had flown very low, just over the heads of the women, and were a very strong hint to them to say nothing. Mrs. Smith merely glanced at them, and showed no surprise when Bert appeared out of the forest holding a spear. His bow was slung over his shoulder, leaving his left arm free, and the light sharp flint of the spear shone in what was left of the firelight, so menacing and so close that, when Bert lifted a finger of his left hand to his lips, the spear seemed to have said already all that that sign would say. Mrs. Smith said never a word, nor did her daughters.

"Come," said Bert to Kate. And Kate rose up and walked towards the spear, and none of the women moved. And before the gypsy men knew that anything had occurred, she and Bert were several yards away in the forest, whose darkness cloaked them completely. A girl slipped round to the shelter of the other side of the oak and ran to tell the gypsy men what had happened, and they came running to take counsel of Mrs. Smith. But she pointed to where her crystal lay wrapped in old silks beside her.

"It was all there in the crystal," she said. "I did not look; but it was all there. It was to be."

Chapter XVIII

There are so many things to do living mostly alone in a small house, that I almost forgot Kate. The details of what I was doing all the morning may not interest my reader, and they are in any case unconcerned with the futuroscope; but, uninteresting though they may be, they occupied me all the morning and for some of the afternoon, and I was not free to turn my attention to that far future, to see if Bert got Kate safe away from the gypsies, until well on toward evening. Then I went to the futuroscope and turned the light on where I had left it, where Sydenham clothed with forests rose like an island promontory above the great London crater, with the waters of it flashing as far as the eye could see. The light showed up the old beeches and oaks once more, now clear in the daylight with some of their mystery gone, and the wretched little hut with its crude forge that had so horrified Kate. The gypsies were still there, resting their tired pony, which, loose and unbridled, was grazing along one of the glades. The disk of the futuroscope took in the whole of the encampment, and I saw at once that Kate was not with the gypsy women or anywhere in the camp. Lee was sitting upon a fallen trunk, playing his pipe of reed. Something in his face and something in his tune seemed to say that the past was past, and that of all the things that were lost in it none were brighter than what were to be found in the future. Mrs. Smith looked completely resigned, and the younger women were all busy tending small fires and cooking. The children were all at play. Then, satisfied that Kate had escaped from her captors, I brought the luminous disk back over the hills and into the hut in the Darenth valley, not far from my house or from the very machine that was creating that light, if you measure by hundreds of yards; otherwise something over five hundred years away.

I narrowed the disk and brought it inside the hut. There I saw Maud spreading dough on one of the clay pans, and Liza grinding corn in a hollowed stone by turning another stone round and round inside it; and a look at the flour she ground, so different from what we grind with our great machines, set me thinking, and it was some while before I turned the disk outside the hut to see if Bert had come home. But there was no sign of him. I saw all the others, Joe with the sheep, Alf feeding the pigs in the sty, and Bill with a small bow, hoping to shoot a pigeon. I looked in all their faces, but could see no trace of anxiety about Bert. So I roamed the light over the hills, whose outlines I know so well, and it was curious to see them so little changed in so very long, as it seems to us. But what are a few centuries to the hills? Any changes I saw were no more than a slight blurring of a few of their outlines by somewhat more wood than there was in my time, which is today. And the village was gone, which they sheltered. Of course I need not have wondered at their holding their shape through all those years. They only heave and sink with millions of years; never with centuries. So there they all stood in the sun, dressed in their natural dress of scabious and roses, and crowned with forest scarred once by the streets of cities, but all those scars were healed, their faint lines showing no more on the face of the hills than old scratches of thorns on the face of a hunting man.

And just as I was going to turn to the hut again, two figures came out of the wood and together strode down the hill that slopes to the Darenth. Then they came out of the shadow of the hill that was now hiding the sun, and its low rays shone in their hair and glowed on their faces, I saw they were Bert and Kate. Soon they had crossed the Darenth and come to the hut. They entered the hut and for a while I saw no more of their radiant faces. Of the marriage customs of these people I knew nothing; indeed I knew very little of them at all, only picking up bits of information about them here and there from occasional guesses that I was able to make from such glimpses as I had leisure to get through the futuroscope. But it was clear enough to me, and would have been to anybody who saw them, that whatever customs they had, Bert and Kate were going to get married.

For a while I watched the rays of the sun slanting over that peaceful valley, gilding the fleeces of sheep and flashing upon the trees that crown the hills on the opposite side from the one behind which the sun was now sinking, old forests of beech-trees, with yews all dark among them, more ancient, as it seemed, than even the beeches, and sometimes whitebeams gaily waving beside them the sudden flash of the under side of their leaves whenever a breeze turned them. And wherever the hills were bare on that side of the valley, the dry stalks of the grasses were now turning gold. From this lovely scene mere curiosity brought me back to the hut to hear Kate's story of her captivity with the gypsies, which I felt so sure of hearing as soon as I picked her up with the futuroscope. And as soon as I did get the luminous disk right into the hut by the Darenth, I heard her indignant voice, but telling Maud and her daughter not so much of her captivity as of the dreadful things she had seen while the gypsies' captive, their accursed place in the wood. For that little forge of theirs, or anything that had to do with taking its shape from metal and moulding it to men's fancies, was clearly to her a sacrilege. It seemed silly to me, but to her it must have seemed that Watt and Stephenson, and whatever magicians she thought had ruined our era, were standing just round the corner waiting for the smelting of a few bits of metal to invent machines that would ruin her civilization. Civilization may be the wrong word for those little huts and their sheepfolds and pigsties, but it was all, no doubt, the way of the world to them, as our way of doing things is to us. She poured out her indignation to Maud and Liza.

Lore does not give reasons and, where it condescends to details, it chooses its own, leaving out many that would be guideposts to reason, and the lore that had been handed down and had reached Kate only seemed to have told that there was a curse in the heart of metal and that it should be left brooding and harmless there in each lump of iron ore that lay on the downs, and never disturbed from its rest by bellows and fire with rites that to her were merely Satanic, or the work of whatever gods of evil she feared. The lore that those people handed down and taught must have simply told that the removal of metal from its natural shapeless state to shapes that some of them sometimes saw lying under the moss was a deed that had darkened the past and, whatever terrible things it had done, the smelting of a few bits of iron might immediately do it again. It is not that they regretted our civilization, some shape of the fragments of which they saw lying under long mounds, but it had been handed down to them that something had shattered it, and they feared that what shattered our way of life could as easily shatter theirs.

"They were doing the accursed thing in the wood," said Kate. For ignorant though she was of the rudiments of our machinery, she could see that the metal was glowing and changing its shape, and knew, as the first men to make a horseshoe never knew, something of what it all led to, even though she knew no more than I exactly what it was that had caused the great London crater. Then Joe and Alf came in, and soon after them Bill, and of course Toby, and they all welcomed Kate. And soon she was pouring out her indignant tale again of the sacrilege that the gypsies were committing on the high ground to the west. They all knew definitely that the crater had been caused by disaster, and, whatever the disaster was, they feared that the gypsies might bring it again. All of them spoke so much of their horror at what the gypsies were doing, and of their fears of what it would bring, that I could not clearly hear them. But Joe stood and said nothing. And after a while he said: "We must ask the Seer of Canterbury."

So Canterbury had its sanctity still, and for a moment that surprised me. And then I remembered that it was only five or six centuries across which I was looking, which was no more than a quarter of the time since the first church was built there, and, whether or not the cathedral was standing still, the sanctity of the place had evidently endured. They stopped talking when Joe spoke, and then he said to Alf: "Run over to Canterbury and tell the Seer there is sacrilege over there to the west."

When he said, "Run over to Canterbury," I remembered that the distance was about forty miles, but this did not seem to trouble Alf, and he went at once to pick up a few provisions of bread and cheese, and was soon off with his spear and bow on the long journey. I looked at their faces and could see the same expression of horror on all of them, an expression aware that only a little way over the western horizon the first step was being taken, even then, in a process of which they knew nothing but that it would ruin the world.

Chapter XIX

I tell of changes so momentous, of such convulsions to our earth and our history, that readers of these notes I have jotted down will be sure to look for events more serious than those that interest me. And were it not that those events affected the course of my narrative I should hesitate to record them. What happened was that the charwoman, who always comes up from the village on Thursdays, did not come on the day following that on which I watched Alf run from the hut on his way to Canterbury. It was a Thursday, and she should have come. I waited all the morning, and then saw that her neglected duties would fall on me. This, however trifling may appear the details of what I had to do, gave me an arduous day's work. Not only this, but I could not work with the pace and accuracy with which the charwoman does, and this meant that I was kept occupied for the whole of the next day. It had not occurred to me, and so may not occur to my reader, that charring is a definite occupation, and that, as with all occupations, those who practise it are more adroit at it than any of those who do not. I had not thought of that, but I found that it was so, and so much so that by the end of the second evening I had scarcely finished what she could have done that day. And so it was late on the morning after that when I returned to my borrowed futuroscope. I had oiled the knobs and dusted it, but no more than that for three days. Now I turned it on to the valley again where the hut of Joe and Maud stands near the Darenth. They were both inside the hut, and seemed to be talking anxiously. None of the others was inside. The Wild Man had come in the night and leaned over the pen and seized a sheep, probably by the scruff of its neck, and had gone away to eat it, and this was what they were talking about. Their anxious faces told me that the Wild Man was a menace, one of the many menaces among which their lives were spent, and they seemed troubled not only by the loss of their sheep, but as to whether the Wild Man would come again. It was strange to hear them speak of the Wild Man, for to me they seemed so wild themselves, a family, and I suppose a whole population, without even any metal. They were practically a neolithic people, and yet they spoke of a wild man. And wild he certainly was.

Then I turned the light out of the hut and widened it and ran it along the valley to see what the others were doing. Bert was watching the sheep on the side of the hill and I saw no sign of Kate, and Alf had not yet returned. And then, as I picked up Liza and Bill just outside the hut, I saw them both looking up the valley, and, turning the place-knob to follow their gaze, I saw two figures coming out of a clump of willows far up the Darenth. It seemed that Liza and Bill had recognized them already, but I could not. My eyesight is not quite what it was, but it never had the keenness of these people, whose eyes were focussed not to the pages of books or papers nor even to neighbouring walls, but to horizons. The two came striding on, one young, one old, but both keeping a good pace. One had a grey beard and wore a cloak and carried a long staff. The smaller and younger one was dressed in skins, and after a while I saw what Bill and Liza had seen at once, that he was Alf. So the other one with him was the Seer of Canterbury, and he had come all the way from his home.

When the circle of the futuroscope with which I was following them included Liza and Bill I saw that they were surprised and excited to see the Seer there. They knew of Alf's message, but had not seemed to think that the great man would have come to see them. They called to their father, and he and Maud came to the door of the hut, and there they welcomed the Seer of Canterbury when he arrived with Alf, and they all went into the hut and I narrowed the luminous disk and followed them in with it, and the Seer spoke.

"Is it true what I have been told," he asked Joe, "that they meddle with metal in the woods of Sydenham?"

I was astonished to hear him call the place Sydenham. And yet I should not have been, for the name had only had to come down five or six hundred years from the time I knew it, I mean from now, and it had come down much longer already from who knows when, and many a name has come from far longer.

Joe nodded his head.

"I have come from Canterbury to warn you," said the Seer, "that the place where they do it must be destroyed. It is accursed, and will bring a curse on the world."

Joe bowed his head again, and the other three were silent.

"This has been done before," went on the Seer, "the story has been handed down to us. Metal turned from its own shape is still lying under the soil, all ruined. You must destroy their accursed place or it will ruin us all, as those who lived with the old iron were ruined."

Then he turned round and walked out of the hut. I moved the light of the futuroscope into the open air and saw him striding away by the way he had come, eastwards towards Canterbury. I ran the light back to the hut to hear what they were saying there. But they said very little. What the Seer had said was evidently a command to them, and Joe was silent and thoughtful. They had evidently already decided to send for Bert, for Bill had slipped out of the hut and the slightest touch on the place-knob showed him running up the hill to where Bert was watching the sheep. So little were they saying in the hut that I decided to have my lunch and to continue my curious eavesdropping on the far future after I had finished, by which time I was sure that Bill would have come back with Bert. And I wanted to hear where Kate was, and how her and Bert's plans for happiness prospered. So I had lunch and then made some coffee and went back to the futuroscope with my cup of coffee on the table beside it. I like it what is sometimes oddly called "white", that is to say with some milk and sugar in it. One glance I took out of the window at the tidy hills that we know, sheltering an old village, then I turned to the futuroscope and switched the light on. And there were the same hills, so different and yet so unaltered, like an old friend wearing a completely new dress. I took a sip of my coffee; then narrowed the disk and turned it inside the hut. Joe was giving his orders to Bert, which the rest had already heard, and Bert had evidently just arrived in the hut, having put the sheep in their pen already, for I heard all of them baaing as though a little surprised at being taken from their hill slopes so early, which I realized had to be if Bert had to come to the hut, because those times were too wild for sheep to be unwatched on the hills. Our days too can be wild, but not all the time, like theirs. Bert wanted to marry Kate, all he said was directed towards that end, and all he thought. And I could easily see what he thought, for his thoughts were very transparent. But his father said that he could not marry until they had destroyed the accursed place of the gypsies, where iron was twisted out of its natural shape to do harm to the world.

"Only a few little pieces," said Bert, "I could see them."

But Joe was fortified by the words of the Seer himself, corroborating and giving authority to whatever lore had already been handed down to him, and he said, "It is the beginning. But it all leads to the things that are buried under those mounds."

Some word Bert muttered in extenuation of what lay under the mounds, not because he knew anything of them or cared what had been their fate, but because he wanted at least to delay while he married Kate. But his father said: "Those things ruined themselves and all who depended on them."

And against this Bert found nothing to say, but only asked to be allowed to go over the hill to see Kate once more, where she had evidently gone back to her father's hut, which was in the direction of Halstead. But his father said, "No. We must destroy that place first. One never knows with beginnings. At any moment they may get so far that there is no turning back from them."

Bert gave a sigh and resigned himself. Then their talk was of weapons and of provisions, and I saw that they were not starting immediately on their journey to the wooded promontory overlooking the great London crater. So I switched off the light for the day, and several times I switched it on again the following morning and found they had not yet started. But about noon when I switched it on I did so just at the right moment and found they were all leaving the hut, with the exception of Maud and her daughter and Bill and the dog. They set out at a pace with which I should never have been able to keep up, a good five miles an hour, and uphill, in the direction in which the sun sets at this time of year, that is to say roughly northwest. I followed them with the light and watched them as they went, taking more note of them than I should have been able to do had I been pacing beside them. They all had bows swung beside them with the bowstrings across their chests, and Bert and Alf carried spears and their father an axe, spearheads and axe-heads all made of grey flint dimpled with hollows from which flakes had been driven off. From the left side of all three hung leather quivers, well filled with arrows slung by strips of leather from their right shoulders. They were all dressed in brown deerskins and their feet were wrapped in hides that were strapped round them to make what some might call boots and, some, sandals. They wore no hats, and their light brown hair showed clear in my luminous disk. All the way over a valley where the village used to lie, and up the slope of the hills, they walked over open grasses faintly rippled by the graves of old streets, for London had once come out all that way, but near the top of the hill they entered the forest and I was still able to follow them, dodging among the trees just as they did. They were going by the way the gypsies had taken, which was far to the right of Halstead. On their left there lay in the forest a district known to me as Rodgers Mount, full of villas and gardens now, but obviously once a home of the badgers, and I saw from great holes in the sand as I turned the place-knob that it was the home of badgers again. Then we came to a valley, with sides too steep for trees, and it was all a garden of flowers. Joe and his two sons climbed down the side and up the opposite one, knowing no more of the origin of that strange valley than we guess what old earthquakes once shaped the valleys we know. But I knew: it was a cutting of the Southeastern railway, the one that runs to Dover. Here, when they had climbed out of the cutting, Bert could not help looking to his left, for over there was the hut in which Kate lived with her father. And suddenly he turned to his father and said: "We are only three, and there are so many of the gypsy men. Shall I get Bob?"

And I understood from the direction in which he glanced that by Bob he meant Kate's father. This was a suggestion, as Bert must have known, that his father could not easily reject. For a moment Joe hesitated, knowing that Bert's motive was to see Kate; but he must have realized the advantage of an addition to his little force, for he agreed to let Bert go, and I heard him arrange a meeting place with Bert, which was to be at a point on the gypsies' track through the forest when they left the lower ground about Southend Lane and began to climb towards Sydenham, beyond which was nothing but the lake of the crater. Bert went off at once, travelling with the ease of a wild animal over towards Halstead; but when he got outside my luminous disk I kept it on Joe and Alf and followed them through the forest on their way to Greenstreet Green. And presently at the ends of glades I could see to their left the flash of the waters of the great London crater, and saw a flight of swans fly over the forest towards that great expanse. Joe and Alf were moving slower now, evidently so as to give Bert time to come up with his reinforcement, and before they came to the meeting place they had arranged they sat down and ate bread and cheese. I could have looked long at them in that forest of the future full of foxgloves and rose-willow, with butterflies flashing as they floated through sunbeams that came down through gaps in the foliage and warmed the sand, but I had other things to do.

So I disconnected the futuroscope while I attended to them, and did not turn it on again until I calculated there was time for Bert to come up with Kate's father. I got the futuroscope working again late in the afternoon and, turning the luminous disk on to the place where I had last left it, I found that Joe and Alf had gone on; so I followed along the track until I came to them. I had calculated pretty accurately; for, when I picked them up, they were just approaching the meeting place they had arranged at the bottom of the hill going up to Sydenham, and Bert and Kate's father had arrived there before them. They were actually now on the tracks of the cart-wheels of the gypsies. Kate's father, Bob, had a large bow of old yew wood in his hand and had slung from his shoulder a quiver full of arrows fletched with swan's feathers, and carried no other weapon. If he was rather too old for fighting with a spear, he had with his old bow the air of a man who had been an archer in his youth. When they went on he walked behind the others, just as artillery in our day would go behind the bayonets. The discovery that yew made the best bows would not have been handed down from our time, for we have forgotten the bow. It must have been something those people had learned for themselves, or rather an old lesson they had been taught newly by Mother Earth. Indeed these people had no-one else to teach them, for I saw no signs of any lore that had come down from before the time of the great London crater, except some things that the gypsies seemed to have remembered and which the rest regarded with horror, and which these four were now setting out to destroy. The gypsies had at least six fully grown men and one or two more women than men, and the rest were children. So that the addition of the old archer was a valuable reinforcement and the odds were no longer two to one.

As they climbed higher up through the forest they went more cautiously, often stopping to listen. I followed them, listening too, keeping the luminous disk on them all along the sandy track. The further they got the more excited I became, as I wondered what would happen, and I wanted to run the light on ahead to see where the gypsies were, but did not do so because I did not like to lose sight of the four men. As they went on through the wood and still saw no sign of the gypsies I glanced at the beauty of the scene around them, the great trunks of the trees framing a small picture, but one full of so much. Foxgloves raised the spires of their delicate flowers, whose brilliant pink glowed in the wood, an unrivalled colour, till we came to the patches of tall rose-willow which seemed just to outshine it. And here and there glided above them, and in and out of the trees, umber butterflies with white spots on their wings which in the sunlight flashed like specks of the sunlight itself. And the song of the thrushes set it all to music. I could have looked long on this scene through which the four men were moving, but my eye was suddenly caught by the trunk of an oak I remembered, and I saw that we were close to the forge of the gypsies, that link between the age of iron and the age of stone that had returned, and which the four men regarded with such enmity.

"It is here," said Bert. And I saw in the faces of all of them that this was the fortress of an enemy that threatened their country and, to their way of thinking, the whole world. I looked about to see where the forge was, and so did they; but there were only the foxgloves. This seemed to me to make the place even more ominous. If the forge was hidden, might not the gypsies be hidden? And I feared a flight of arrows from behind any of the trees that surrounded us. A foolish fear, I admit, for I was over five hundred years from those gypsies, wherever they were; but most fears are foolish. Joe and his two sons moved forward very cautiously, and old Bob remained behind with a long arrow fitted to his bowstring. Bert was leading the way, searching carefully, and watching just as carefully for any sign of a gypsy and listening for any sound of them. Still he saw nothing but those myriad foxgloves, and the great oaks looking down on them.

"It was here," he said, standing still. And from what I could remember I thought he was right; but there was no sign of any hut or the forge that it had contained. And then the old archer came up to him.

"Come back tomorrow," he said, "and dig where the foxgloves are drooping."

Chapter XX

I switched off the light when I heard the words of the old man, for I had seen that, wherever the forge had gone, it was completely hidden, and I decided to look again when they dug next day following the old man's advice. What time of day that would be I had no way of knowing, but that did not trouble me, for all I had to do was to leave the place-knob where it was and take a glimpse at the forest whenever I had leisure to do so. I turned on the light several times during the morning and they were not there, nor was there a sign of any gypsy. And then after my lunch, as I was drinking a cup of coffee at my table in the window, at which the futuroscope stands, I connected it up again and saw all four men just arriving, armed as they had been before and also carrying two spades. The wooden shafts of the spades were not much unlike ours, but the spades themselves looked very odd to me and appeared to be made out of the horns of fallow deer. As the men looked through the wood I looked too, and I think all of us saw about the same moment a clump of foxgloves whose flowers had all lost their lustre and were drooping from the stem rather than leaning out from it, and were sagging so that they seemed narrower than those that were blooming round them.

I saw now the sense of the old man's suggestion, for these flowers had clearly been tampered with, so that whatever had been buried and perfectly concealed yesterday could be traced today by anyone looking carefully. And here Bert and Alf began to dig, while the old archer watched, with his arrow still on the bowstring. They had not dug for long, when they began to uncover an old piece of iron that took the shape of an anvil as the sand was cleared away from it, and must have been an anvil of our time, or perhaps a little before it, for forges are growing scarce with us now, which the gypsies must have dug up, since I had seen no trace of anything in England, as I saw it through the futuroscope, that could have made anything like that. The bellows came up next, and these I saw at a glance the gypsies had made themselves from the skin of an animal and pieces of wood and crude bits of metal which they could have been able to smelt. Then came their tongs and their hammers, and the collection was mostly very much what some archeologist might have dug up from an encampment of the dawn of the iron age, which is about where these gypsies were, while the age of the four men bent on destroying these things as infamous implements of sacrilege was neolithic.

We have rivalries among schools and universities, but these are friendly, and we have rivalries among nations, which are bitter; but I was learning now that the bitterness of any rivalries of ours is far surpassed by the bitterness among ages. I saw this from the fury with which they broke up all these tools and the horror with which they looked at them. But more than break them they could not do, and the dark iron lay where they threw it, seeming to threaten their age as the first pieces of metal ever smelted must have threatened the stone age. Then they picked up the pieces of metal and threw them still further away, scattering them through the wood and seeming to pick them up hastily, as though awed by the mere touch. With the anvil they could do nothing and left it lying there, a piece of the ruin of an age that was lost. Then abruptly they turned from the place that to them was clearly accursed for the sake of the traffic that it had had with the things of an age of which they knew nothing, and against which some old lore of theirs only warned them. In whatever lore may have survived at Canterbury there may have been something more, but all these people knew was that there had been an age that had twisted metal from its intended shapelessness to make things out of harmony with the woods and the hills, and that this age had ruined itself and the woods had survived. It was little to know, but whatever knowledge they had they clung to fiercely, and these four were now doing what they could to prevent a return of a civilization that they had been taught was accursed.

Still no gypsies returned, the four men could do no more, and they started homeward through the summer gloaming on what to us would be a long walk. They walked for miles through the forest, with birds singing as they sing now, and, coming down from a promontory above Farnborough that stood by the edge of the crater, they divided, Bert and the father of Kate turning to their right and going along the shore of the lake, and Joe and Alf recrossing the flowery valley which had been a cutting of the Southeastern railway, and going through Chelsfield back to their home by the Darenth, which they reached before stars were shining or wolves were abroad. The old archer with his big bow brought Bert back to his reed-hung hut sooner than that, and Kate and Bert went up to the slope again between the lake and the forest, to watch the glow that was hanging over the sunset as colour went out of the earth and into the sky; and they watched the bats drawing their black lines across the shining colour, and apparently a great many more things than what I could see, for there was a continual delight in their eyes. They spoke of their coming marriage and I listened awhile to find if I could learn anything of what the marriage ceremonies of those people were, but they said nothing of them that was at all clear. And then that feeling which I had had before that I was eavesdropping came over me again, and I left them happy under the Evening Star. One glance I took at the other two, and saw them actually crossing the Darenth at a ford within barely a mile of their hut and, thinking that there could be nothing more of interest there, I thought of my own supper and disconnected the futuroscope while I had it.

I had a good supper after my day's work, for that is what it felt like. I know that it is absurd to speak of work when all I did was to keep my eye at a circular glass and watch other men working, while I only occasionally gave almost imperceptible touches to a well-oiled knob. But I felt tired, for all that. My mind had covered the distance of a very long walk and back again and had been filled with impressions of beauty with which the forest glades had abounded, and I felt actually fatigued by it all. So I intended to take no more than a glance at the futuroscope that night. I turned the light on to the hut by the Darenth for no particular reason, except that that was the start of my journeys into the future, and there I expected to see Joe and Alf resting after their long expedition and telling of what they had done. But as soon as I turned the light on the hut I found all was confusion. Joe and Alf had just arrived and they and Maud were all talking at once, and Liza had gone. Among all their excited voices, which rather jarred the futuroscope speaking all together, I heard two words often repeated, the Wild Man. He had come through the woods again shouting, as Maud said, and Bill said he was singing. Bill's version of what happened was the first clear one I heard.

"When I heard him I got your big bow," he said, "and stood by the door to protect Liza. There was still light enough to shoot by, and I had an arrow ready. But then Liza went out to hear him singing. I told her not to."

"She was gone before I could stop her," said Maud. "She must have been mad."

I could not question them across all those ages, and never heard quite what had happened. But the Wild Man had got Liza. Their plans were clearer to me than their story of what had happened. They did not yet know where the Wild Man had gone, except that he had gone off to the south. Bill had not seen him, because he had not come out of the wood, to the edge of which Liza had so rashly gone, and Toby had remained guarding the hut and had not hunted the Wild Man. Joe decided that they must track him by daylight, when he would be helpless against their arrows, and not by night, when everything in the forest went in fear of him. They would need Bert; and Joe set off at once with his spear and bow, and the horn slung from his shoulder in case of wolves, in order to bring Bert. For a long while I followed Joe through the forest to see if he would get through it safely. And in safety he traversed it, and I gathered that the wolves had learned a hard lesson. By starlight he came to the old man's hut, and I manoeuvred the light inside it as he entered, and there were Bert and Kate and her father all sitting by the hearth, on which a small fire was glowing. It was getting late, and I only stopped to hear what they were going to do; and Joe's plans for that made me think of the old adage which says that the course of true love never did run smooth. For as soon as it was light enough for them to be able to see to protect themselves against wolves Joe said that Bert must come back with him to his hut by the Darenth, in order to track the Wild Man and rescue Liza. I stopped to hear no more, for whatever regrets I saw in the faces of Kate and Bert, I could see that Joe was the dominant character in that hut, and Kate's father had little to say. So I switched off the futuroscope and went to bed.

As soon as I had had breakfast next morning I connected up the futuroscope again and turned it on to Joe's hut. I was just in time, and they were already setting out, Joe, Bert and Alf, and Toby; and only Maud remained in the hut with Bill, who had been given a big bow with which to guard the hut and look after the sheep, to console him for not being allowed to take part in the wild-man-hunt. They moved up the slope at once to the wood, evidently making for a certain spot at which the Wild Man had been heard, for Maud stood outside the hut as though to direct them. But they must have gone into the wood at exactly the right spot, for she never called. I followed them there, and they found a broken twig and then looked for a track, and for a while they seemed to follow one, though I could not see any track myself; and soon they appeared at a loss, and, the scent being long cold, Toby could not help them. They were moving through the wood towards the south, the direction from which the Wild Man had always come, but they were going hesitatingly and spreading out and searching for something they could not find, and that Toby could not scent. They all had horns as well as Joe's axe and the sharp flint spears of Bert and Alf. All the morning they were searching for tracks, but found no more than the one they had followed for such a little way. Sometimes one called to the others because he had found a foxglove broken or a piece of moss disturbed from a stone or a fallen leaf, or something that I could not see at all, but they never picked up a track again, and Toby sniffing at every tree and stone could not find anything either. I felt as excited as they must have been when they started out to rescue Liza. But I could not keep up my interest all the morning after they lost the track, and I left them searching through the wood and only switched on every now and then to see if they had found anything. And they found nothing, and moved a long way away to the south, so far that sometimes it took me a minute or so to pick them up again. They knew the direction from which the Wild Man always came, but had nothing else to guide them. Along that line they moved away rather in the direction of Sussex. Still they found nothing.

Chapter XXI

That afternoon I ran the luminous disk back to the Darenth valley and turned it inside the hut, I believe with some idea of telling Maud that the men had not yet been able to pick up the track of the Wild Man. Of course the moment I got the light into the hut and saw Maud sitting disconsolate there, I realized quickly enough that I could not speak to her across five or six hundred years. But, living so much with the futuroscope as I have been doing for the last few weeks, I feel so close to that family that I often get these fancies. The ground on which their hut stands is under a mile from me where I sit at my window, and all the scenery is my scenery, although so much altered by forest; and the futuroscope brings me so close to that family, that I often forget that when I am only a yard or so from them they are nearly six centuries away from me. As I have said before, it is very confusing. And yet, in spite of all the things that often confuse me, I want to record what I have seen as clearly and logically as I can, in order to place before the public the pleasures to be derived from a futuroscope. The jar of moving five centuries with the turn of a finger and thumb, the shock of what I may call crossing the time-barrier, are soon got over, and the puzzling difficulty of being unable to say a word to people so close to the user of this interesting machine, whose words he can hear so clearly, is, after all, an inconvenience no greater than that experienced by the owner of a television set. Forcing myself to bear this in mind, I took one more glance at Maud, then ran the light outside, and seeing no sign of the men returning, I switched it off.

All that evening I pictured the three men going further and further south on their long hunt, looking for tracks that they seemed so unlikely to find. Once more I turned on the futuroscope, to look for them after I had had my dinner, and found that that was what they had been doing; for, moving the disk southwards, I came on a fire they had evidently lit to keep away wolves, and they and Toby were lying down beside it, Toby with his head on his paws, looking into the fire with great contentment. As they were evidently doing no more that night, I switched off again. And later that evening the idea came to me that I was far better equipped to look for the Wild Man than they were. So next morning I turned the futuroscope on to the same place, where the ashes of their fire were all grey, and found the three men and the dog had already gone on southwards. And southwards I went too with my luminous disk, and soon overtook them, spread out and searching for tracks. It was a huge cast they were making, and I could not think they had much chance of success, looking for one wild man and his captive in all that forest. So I ran the light on before them right through the forest and out to the South downs, perhaps hoping to find him there for no better reason than that one so like him had once roamed over those downs and had his mighty portrait left on a hill. A poor enough reason, and, let me admit it, my whole search was useless; for, if I did find him, how could I put his pursuers on the right line? And I hunted over those downs all the way to the sea and came back through the forest again, and did not find him. Nor did the three men and their dog, for I came on them again still going southwards on my way back.

I think, as I drifted the luminous disk through the forest and out of it to the grassy slopes of the downs, I was led back by some vague impulse to see Maud again and to tell her that her husband had not been able to find the Wild Man. Of course it was a foolish impulse, as it was totally impossible for me to speak to her, but I think that that, if anything, was what was directing me as I twiddled the place-knob. I wonder if fancies as foolish as that can ever come to people sitting beside their television sets and watching some figure as close as I was able to watch those in that hut. Probably, for we all have foolish fancies at times, and ghosts of fancies, mere shadowy impulses that we cannot define and which sometimes we do not even know to be driving us. But whatever trivial fancies were driving me, I was bringing the luminous disk back to the hut, and was barely two miles away from it, when I saw a patch of kingcups flashing back sunlight beside a little stream that trickled into the Darenth, and I narrowed the light to look at their beauty more closely in a flat meadow lying between two lines of hills. And as I idly brought my eye to the kingcups I saw two round marks on the mud by the little stream, which attracted my attention. And as I tried to make out what they were, I saw clearly a giant footprint, one print of a huge foot. And I saw it must have been made by the Wild Man. No-one else that I had seen in that far future, except the gypsies' children, went barefooted, and no-one else was as huge. I looked attentively, but could find no footprints and, examining the great circles in the mud and picking up less clear traces of great fingers and toes, I saw that he must have been drinking there.

    I cast all over the field then, to see which way he had gone, and for a long while could get no more tracks, and indeed got no more definite tracks at all, but I did come on some broken rushes further away and, by examining them closely, saw that the Wild Man was going in the same direction as I, that is to say into the Darenth valley. The tracks were fairly fresh, and that puzzled me. For what could he want with the hut, now that

Liza was gone? And the track through the rushes appeared to be heading straight towards it. I could not track like Joe and his sons, and a bent blade of grass or a broken flower which would have guided them meant nothing to me. And so it was more luck than woodcraft, indeed almost purely luck, that suddenly brought me on him where three men and a dog had failed. For when I was only a mile away from the hut, coming along the grassy slope under the forest that clothes the western hill, I suddenly saw the mouth of a huge cave. What great excavation had been made by this folk of the future, I wondered? And all of a sudden I remembered. It was the southern end of the tunnel on the railway that runs to Dover, the long tunnel from Halstead to Twitton. And here where the train used to emerge into daylight the mouth of the tunnel still gaped at the hills. Huge curtains were hung across it, not by Man but by Nature; and clematis, Traveller's Joy, made a fringe to cover the top of it and draped the whole of both sides; but, lower down, skins were hanging from long poles.

So vast was the screen of skins which sheltered the great cave from the wind, and so huge were the poles that supported it, that I saw at once it must be the home of the Wild Man. For somebody huge lived there, and one that was barbarously wild, and only the tanned skins and the cut poles showed me that it was not the lair of a large animal. I glanced round that wild place so strangely draped by Nature, strangely because the tunnel of a great railway seems so remote from Nature and her clematis; and I twisted the luminous disk about the slope of the hill. Ages ago, which is now, there used to be musk orchids all over that slope, and I wondered if I could find any still. They were there in abundance. Six centuries seem so much to us; but it was as though Nature took no heed of them; and it is curious how calmly time seems to lie on the hills, while its waves lash Man so fiercely. It seems like the calm of an ocean, all blue as far as the sky, while just at its edge small waves shift and overturn little things and hurry them up and down; or so it seemed to me as I looked at the great mouth of that tunnel, all in the calm of the hills, and calm now itself under drooping curtains of clematis.

But I had not gone to the future in order to make those reflections. I had gone for the sake of the hunt of the Wild Man, so far as my own amusement was concerned, and had jotted down these notes in order to entertain the reader with the possibilities of the futuroscope and to recommend him to buy one, if the price is reasonable, as soon as a supply of them is put on the market. To turn, then, to my original purpose this morning, which was to take part with the three men and the dog in the hunt for the Wild Man, whose track they had lost, I brought the light back to the mouth of the tunnel and narrowed it and ran it inside. And there I saw the huge nude figure of the Wild Man on a skin that, so far as I could see in the dim light, was that of a red deer. I ran the luminous disk further into the tunnel at once, hoping to find Liza, but though I call the disk luminous, for it actually is, it gives no light to dark places. It is rather no more than a circle of pale colour, marking the area of visibility, but making nothing more visible to me than it is to the people that are actually living with it, or perhaps I should say will be living with it, for it is all in the far future. Well, I ran my pale yellow circle further into the tunnel past a few more hanging skins and great curtains of ivy, and saw some more skins on the floor, but wherever I looked in the dim untidiness I caught no sight of the old rails or sleepers, unless occasional ridges that I traced in the dried mud were any sign of them. How strangely altered it all was from the time when I remembered Pullman cars running through on their way to Dover and flashing out into sunlight just at that spot, or on their way up from Dover disappearing suddenly into the hill. The contrast between the warm and tidy carriages and this dim barbarism was forced on me. Life is perhaps made of contrasts, as all things seen are made of light and shade. A line from an old song hummed in my head, "Where my caravan has rested;" but it was not an appropriate line, for those Pullmans of which I was thinking did not rest there, but rushed through at a mile a minute. All was stagnant there now.

As soon as I left the dim shape of the gigantic figure and passed through the curtain of ivy I saw no more, and could not tell whether Liza was there or not. I listened attentively, but could hear no sound of her. Nor did the Wild Man speak, and I only heard his breathing. Just as the rails and sleepers had gone back to wild earth and ivy, so he had gone back from the clothed people we know, masters of so much power until it fell from their grasp, all the way back to the savagery of the naked man with two sticks, whose portrait an earlier people left on the hill by Wilmington. There he sat now with his two great sticks beside him, without clothes, without boots, without a wireless set, which are so necessary to us, yet evidently attaining contentment without these things, for his savage face looked calmer than some of ours. And this awoke in me a train of philosophy, which would not interest my reader; and in any case it led nowhere. What I had to do was to find Liza. And then all at once the uselessness of my search occurred to me. For if I did find her I could do nothing whatever, and I not only despaired of my search, but began to wonder if I ought to take any interest in these people at all whose lives I could influence in not the slightest degree. Yet to how many people this also applies; people seen in television or on the screen or read of in books, and even nearer than that, often our closest neighbours: I merely continue in order to lay before the public some of the pleasures to be obtained from a futuroscope, even though at this moment I reaped from it nothing but disappointment. I had got too much interested in these people, and it was bitter to feel that, close to them as I was and as though I were living their lives, I could never do anything for them.

Chapter XXII

From the rather mournful reflections with which I closed the last chapter I soon turned to enquiries that were more to the point. How surprising it was, I thought, that while the three men and their dog hunted far down into Sussex, the Wild Man whom they hunted was under two miles from them. And then it occurred to me that Liza could have screamed and could have been easily heard on a still evening by all those in the hut. Why had she not done so, I wondered, if she was there? And if she was not in the Wild Man's cave, where was she? It seemed a mystery that Joe and his sons were likely to solve as soon as I could, if either of us solved it at all. And certainly they were no nearer any solution when next I turned the light of the futuroscope on to their hut that evening and found them just back with their dog, resting on chairs before their fire after their long journey, having accomplished nothing. They were not speaking, but I could see from Maud's face that they had had nothing to tell her which could have brought any hope. For a long while I listened, but still nobody spoke, and I disconnected the futuroscope for the day.

Next morning when I had dusted the futuroscope and oiled its knobs I ran the luminous disk back to the hut again, to see if they had found out that the Wild Man was within a mile of them, but I saw at once from their faces that they had made no progress, and there was no sign of Liza. I experienced once more the despairing wish to call out to them and to tell them, if with only a dozen words, all that they wanted to know, and the realization that I could say no more to them than I could say to people whom I might meet in dreams. So I turned away, as it was no use my staying, and ran the disk over the hills and turned it into the hut of Bob, the old archer, and there was Kate sitting disconsolate. Two mournful pictures are not what I had intended to show when I set out to enumerate the pleasures of a futuroscope; but one unfortunate incident, the abduction of Liza by the Wild Man, accounted for both; for until they could find out by the Darenth that the Wild Man was within a mile or two of them, Joe would not let his son go away to see Kate. The old archer was in his garden, and neither he nor Kate were speaking; and, finding little enough to interest me there, and nothing at all to cheer me, I was about to switch off, when I saw a look in Kate's eyes which caused me to listen, and far away I heard the sound of a pipe.

It was playing no tune I knew and I only heard it faintly, but it was something to know of it that it was an unknown tune, and that knowledge and the strangeness and wildness of it made me sure it was an air of the gypsies, and caused me to suspect that the player was Lee. Kate's expression was rapt, and at the time it struck me as curious that though she dreaded Lee, as I knew well, yet the tune that he was playing had a fascination for her. And nearer it came, although quite slowly, and still Kate sat listening. I wondered what she would do. And then I switched the light off her and ran it towards the sound of that tune. And, sure enough, it was Lee with all the gypsies. They had turned back from the wooded island of Sydenham, for the waters of the great London crater just came all round it, but they could wade through them at one point to come to the promontory of Farnborough, and from there they would have descended to the shore of the crater along which I saw them coming now. Roughly the radius of the crater was from the centre of London to a little short of Halstead, but not all of it was filled with marsh, nor were all of the hills within it entirely wrecked by whatever had made the crater. Many of the gypsies walking behind Lee were singing to the tune that he played, and some of the children were making casts with small rods in the water as they ran along the edge of the rushes. And now the whole caravan was nearing the old man's hut. I ran back the luminous disk to the hut again. I heard Kate call out to her father, "It is Lee," and he came at once from his garden into the hut and picked up his reddish-brown bow.

"No," said Kate and signed to him to put it down. Then she ran out of the hut, and the gypsies had not yet seen her. She ran towards my futuroscope, towards the Darenth valley, but soon slanted towards her left, and about the time that the gypsies would have arrived at her father's hut I saw her enter the curious flowery valley which I knew for the old cutting of the Southeastern railway. Wild-rose-bushes, privet and dogwood had given her just enough cover for her to be able to avoid being seen by the gypsies until she reached that valley and once she had reached it she was hidden from anyone not standing upon its brink. She came no further in this direction, but turned to her right. And then I saw where she was going. For she came to a great cascade of Traveller's Joy gleaming before her from the ground to the skyline, and there the valley ended. She walked up to the lovely curtain of silvery blooms of the clematis and, putting a hand to a great flowery tendril, drew it aside and walked through, and she was in the old tunnel that emerges at Twitton, and which in our time carries the railway that runs to Dover. Of course nothing remained of the rails, and very little of the tunnel; for, being only a few hundred yards from the edge of the water, all its masonry had been shaken by whatever had caused the crater, and large blocks had fallen out of the walls and roof, and roots of trees had come creeping through in their places and came down through the tunnel, clutching at air until they found the floor and gripped the earth again. Light did not come far through that curtain of clematis and screen of the roots of trees. There would have been a dank smell from those roots and from the soil for which they were groping, and perhaps a faint smell of flowers; but that I cannot say, for I was only conscious of the curious absence of any dank scents such as I had always noticed in all other underground places. But sight and sound are all that the futuroscope will carry. Down this dark corridor made partly by the people of one civilization, partly by the ruin that overtook them, and partly by Nature triumphing over their civilization and mercifully hiding its ruin and draping it with flowers, Kate fled from the gypsies and ran towards Twitton. But before she had gone far it became too dark to run over fragments fallen out of the roof and walls and through the veil of tendrils that hung from the roots of trees, and I saw her clambering amongst these great obstacles until it became too dark for me to make her out any more.

Then I turned back to the gypsies to see if they would follow her, for of course they knew of the tunnel quite as well as she did, and it seemed to me a likely place for them to try, when they found she was nowhere near her father's hut. They were all coming up from the lake and looking round and had not yet started to pursue. Would they go to the tunnel, I wondered? If so, I saw no escape for Kate, for, even if the tunnel were open all the way, she had not much start and they could easily run her down. I felt the temptation to do what many perhaps would have done, which was to turn the time-knob on a few hours to see if they were pursuing her. And why not do it, my reader may ask? Simply because I had never formed the habit, that I believe many readers have, of turning to the end of a book to see what happens. I like to watch things consecutively, following the lives of any who have my interest, and to see time unrolling their story. So I watched the gypsies awhile, all looking about them very much like hounds that have overrun the scent and are about to find it again. Then, rather than turn further into the future I ran the luminous disk back to the hut by the Darenth, to see if they had yet found that the Wild Man who had gone off with Liza was under two miles away from them. But a glance showed that they had found nothing. That was clear in their faces, as I picked them up in the hut and round about it and on the slope of the hill among the sheep. Where Joe was out with the sheep he could not have been more than half a mile from the Wild Man. They had clearly not found Liza, and one could see in Bert's face that he was still not allowed to go away over the hill to look for Kate, where he would have looked for her, in her father's hut.

And then as I was running the light all round the hut, picking them up one by one, I saw Bill going off with a small bow through the meadow up the Darenth. Once as a wild duck rose and he drew out an arrow from the quiver he wore I saw that the flint tip of the arrow was sharp and appeared effective. Once more I find myself through force of habit using the word wild, which is an absurd thing to do of anything in this far future which I was watching, where all things were wild. The duck was quite forty yards away when it rose, and Bill had the sense not to shoot. Then he went on up the Darenth. Presently he saw something, though I could not see what, and began to stalk it, which he did as well as a cat or a fox. I watched with interest, because I was watching something far more skilful than any stalking that I could have done myself, had I ever tried. He was crawling up to a clump of privet, with his bow in his left hand and the arrows all in their quiver at his left side. The stalk took a long time, but I watched it all the while for the sake of its craftsmanship. And then he got to the privet, and shot and missed. For the first time then I saw what he had been stalking, a rabbit, for it suddenly sat up. Then Bill shot another arrow and got it through the ribs. Bill ran as fast as he could up to the rabbit, which was kicking convulsively and could not have run away; but he was evidently afraid it might kick down a hole, for there were several near. But he got his rabbit all right. Then he went on upstream. But soon he crossed the Darenth and slanted away to his right. I followed him still, and saw now that, if he kept on in the direction in which he was going, it would bring him straight to the Wild Man's cave. Would he find it, I wondered?

Soon the cave was staring right at him out of the hill, just the thing to attract a boy; but he was evidently looking for more rabbits, and seemed not to be noticing the cave. Soon he drew level with the cave, but some way below it. If only I could draw his attention. But I could do nothing. He crossed the embankment of the old Southeastern railway, to him only a hillock, and went on. I followed him still with the disk, but with little hope that he would find the Wild Man now, or that any of them would rescue Liza. Still less hope had I of it when he saw something to stalk again, which, running the luminous disk on ahead of him, I found to be another wild duck. He went on all fours, and was at once absorbed in the stalk and in nothing else. The duck was among some rushes upon a flash of water, which was either a tiny stream running into the Darenth, or a bit of marsh in a meadow. I despaired of his finding Liza now. But all of a sudden I saw him stop in his stalk and look closely down at the ground. I narrowed the disk and turned it on what he was looking at, and there I saw again the huge bare footprint of the Wild Man. It was pointing in the direction of his cave. Bill looked carefully at it, and then went on. I followed all his slow stalk and, keeping very low, I saw him come right up to a patch of bulrushes, whose huge leaves covered him from the sight of the duck, which was swimming only a few yards on the far side. He moved not only unseen by the duck, but almost soundlessly, and seemed to know all about stalking, young though he was, that a young fish knows about swimming or a young bird about flying. Then he took out an arrow. It was an easy shot and he got the duck. He jumped into the shallow water at once and picked up the duck with his arrow in it, and went back to pick up his rabbit where he had left it by a wild-rose-bush. Then he turned back again and examined the giant footprint. Very carefully he looked at the ground and must have discovered another print which I could not see, for he strode off at once in a new direction, and that direction led straight to the cave, the old tunnel of the Southeastern railway.

Chapter XXIII

It is strange that I should have got so much interested in the fortunes of those few people so many centuries away, and that my anxieties should have been so keen about Kate and Liza. But I did very little in my house that day, except to have hurried meals, and all the rest of the time I was sitting at the futuroscope, sometimes with a cup of coffee on the table beside me, but barely taking my eyes from the instrument even to drink. I switched the disk back now to the northern end of the tunnel, and it was just as I thought, the gypsies had either tracked Kate, or more likely guessed where she had gone, and were all after her, Lee playing his gypsy tune, the children all following him, rather as those of Hamelin followed the pied piper, and he and all the gypsies pouring into the tunnel. Kate had had a good start, but it was too dark for me to see how far she had gone, and soon the gypsies and she were lost to me in the darkness, all except their children, who were playing about outside, having probably been turned back by the gypsy men. Nor did the gypsy women go far into that cavernous place, but all the gypsy men went on with Lee, and his strange tune sounded fainter and fainter until I could hear it no more. I can only lay the advantages of the futuroscope before the public by describing exactly what I heard and saw in it, and while I am doing that it seems to me just as well to describe my own impressions and fancies, however silly some of them may appear.

And just then I admit that a very silly fancy occurred to me; for while I thought of Kate in that dark tunnel with the gypsies behind her and the Wild Man in front it foolishly occurred to me, what if a train should come! Of course the idea was absurd; she was five or six hundred years away, and the tunnel was all blocked with fallen masonry mixed with the roots of trees. And yet as I took my eye from the futuroscope to take a sip at my coffee and then turned it back, I saw for a moment the view today through my window in which the futuroscope stands, and far away to the southwest I could see the very hill through which the railway runs. And just at that moment I saw a burst of white smoke coming out of the hill. It was a train going to Dover. Of course that could have nothing to do with Kate and the gypsies all those centuries away, but my reader will appreciate how confusing it was for me. From that burst of white smoke and the train rushing to Dover I turned my head but a few inches, and I was looking into the futuroscope at the clematis-hung entrance to a dark cavern, and that train that I had seen a moment ago would all be rusted away, or be marked by a few green mounds only discernible by archeologists from those of the mole and from our own graves, and this in a world where no archeologists were. As I glanced at the train it rushed out of sight Doverwards, and as I turned back to the futuroscope it was gone over five hundred years, and with it was gone all its iron and bits of brass and the steel along which it ran, to be mere curios for somebody to dig up, the remnants of an age whose people had so much power that they could no longer control it.

From this train and from these wandering thoughts about it I turned back to peer into the northern end of the tunnel as far as any light strayed through little rents in the vast curtains of clematis, and there I could no longer see anything except the gypsy children playing, and the sound of Lee's flute had quite faded away. So I ran the disk of the futuroscope over to where I had just seen the smoke bursting out of the hill, which is to say to the southern end of the tunnel, so as to see what Bill had found, and feeling a little anxious about the safety of Bill. But Bill could evidently look after himself, for I saw him with his bow in his hand, travelling back down the side of the Darenth with an unmistakable look in his face of having discovered something of which he was running home to tell. As I could see nothing at the far end of the tunnel, and nothing was happening at the nearer end, I had now leisure to examine the countryside, so as to be able to report for those interested in science or history the great changes that had overtaken the landscape. And, even for those not interested in the future, I felt that I could tell a good deal of what England was like in the remote past; for, if there is anything that I have discovered since I borrowed the futuroscope, it is that the past had come back again. I may be told that this is nonsense; but I can only say that I saw it. As a river may flood fields under cultivation, so time seemed to have risen and submerged the centuries now before me with an age that we thought to be lost. So now, I said to myself, I will make some careful observations of the fauna and the flora of the Darenth valley five or six hundred years hence. But I could not do it. I could not give these things the proper attention. My interest had unfortunately strayed away at one moment to the fate of Liza and at another to that of Kate, and it was all getting twisted up with the interests and the anxieties of Bill. It will be said that if I let such trivial interests get in my way I am no suitable person to have been given this rare, and I may almost say unique, opportunity of seeing the future of the world. But there it is. I have not the necessary qualifications; I know nothing of science or history; and all I can do is to tell a simple tale about a few very simple people.

I disconnected the futuroscope soon in order to have my tea, which at this time of the afternoon is naturally an interest in this age, while in that other age I knew that Bill would be approaching his home to give them all his news. I had my tea and picked up the day's paper, at which I had not yet looked. But the words that I read seemed to have no meaning for me till I read them a second time, and I could not remember them even then, because my interest was so far away. So back I went to the futuroscope and switched it on to that hut which is only a mile from my window; which I mean will be only a mile from my window in over five centuries time. But then my window will no longer be there; so that that statement is not true either. It is indeed very confusing. Well, I switched the futuroscope on and Bill had returned, and all the family were talking hard, too fast for me to hear what they said and all but Maud were picking up bows and spears, and Bill still clung to his bow. Bows seemed to me unlikely to be of any use, since anything I expected to happen seemed likely to take place in the dark of the tunnel. Spears were another matter and those heavy heads of sharp flint five inches across and nearly a foot long seemed formidable weapons.

As I watched them all setting out for the rescue of Liza along that peaceful stream, I became acutely aware of two defects in the futuroscope: one was that in the darkness, such as lay in the tunnel to which Joe and his sons were going, its disk could show me nothing, and the other was that while I watched a crisis flowering in the life of Kate I could see no more of her thoughts than I could see the shapes of anyone in the tunnel. What material for a novelist is cast down before me! How he would tell of Kate's romantic thoughts and the very beats of her heart, her love, her anxiety and her fears! And of all these I know nothing. But it is the same wherever I turn; history, sociology, politics; I know nothing of any of them, and could only describe the glimpses of things I saw in the valley of the Darenth about five hundred years hence and the few people that wandered its hills, over which a great city had spread and had been weighed down by strange snow. Over the streets of that city, the little band I was following now with the luminous disk walked as unheeding of what lay under the ripples of grass, as we of this twentieth century walk over the fields of Romney Street, which lies at the back of these hills and is so named because across it somewhere, I don't know where, ran the hard road from Dover to London along which Julius Caesar marched. What an empire he held! What an empire we held! Well, well.

Chapter XXIV

That was a long day. I could not leave the tunnel and that distant century. If I turned the futuroscope off, there was nothing in my house that could interest me. I could not even read a paper without wondering what had become of Liza and how Kate was faring. And Kate I always thought of first of all, because I had seen her sitting on that sunny slope so happy with Bert, and with him seeming to share the happiness of the butterflies that floated round them upon the summer air and the songs of the birds that sang to her. For no better reason than that. And if I expose these trivial interests of mine to the scorn of all historians, who will wonder, if any should read of them, that with all those centuries of English history laid out before me I could concern myself instead with the wandering fancies of two such primitive girls, it is because I wish to lay before the public all that the futuroscope is able to show, however unimportant those things may be. It is for the purchaser of one of these instruments, whenever they shall be on the market, to study whatever it may reveal to him with more serious purpose then ever comes natural to me. History, politics, sociology, and I know not what other serious studies, can, I feel sure, be enriched by this instrument by anybody fitted for those pursuits; I merely tell what saw.

No sooner had I switched off the luminous disk from Joe and his three sons as they went towards Twitton, than I hurried it up to the northern end of the tunnel to see what I could pick up about Kate. The gypsies were still all in the dark of the tunnel, at least there were none of them to be seen outside; and there was no sign of Kate. What obstacles there were in the tunnel I could not see, and I could not tell how far Kate was able to penetrate them, or even if there was a way through at all, though the absence of any of the gypsies outside, except their children playing in the sun that shone on the flowery valley through which once ran the Southeastern railway, suggested that there was still a way through the tunnel. I ran my pale-yellow disk into it again, but all was darkness. And then a memory came to me from what seemed hundreds of years away, but was only last week really, a memory of a little tower that stood in a field, a tower that is standing there now I mean, which was a ventilation shaft for the Dover line. Light would come down through that, and I wondered if it was still there. So I ran the luminous disk along the Sevenoaks road, the line of which was still marked by a mass of thorn and briars, to look for that squat round tower which I knew was well in sight of the Sevenoaks road, not a hundred yards to the left of it. The tower was all gone, but so well did I remember where it had stood that I felt sure of finding the place. Again I seem to be boasting of a powerful memory, but I must admit that I only saw that tower last week on a walk that I took one evening over the hill. It stood, I mean stands, in a field outside a wood and, although the wood had encroached over the grass some way, that old ventilation shaft was still outside the wood. I saw first a chunk of bricks that lay in the grass. I could not see the bricks, because they were covered with moss, but their angularity protruded from the gentle curves of Nature and unmistakably told of the work of man.

And then I saw a circle of brambles all running down into the earth like a dark green waterfall. This was where the tower, or chimney, had stood, and light still came down from it into the tunnel. So I ran the disk of the futuroscope down, and, dim though the light was down there, noticed that I should be able to see whomever passed. The only question was whether I was in time to intercept them. The brick tower had mostly fallen inwards and was lying in huge blocks at the bottom of the shaft, with the trailing mass of the brambles nearly touching the tops of them. A glance at the solid ruin and the veils of the roots and brambles assured me that I was in ample time to see the pursuit of Kate, for I had come on a good mile from the entrance to the tunnel, and the progress of Kate fleeing and the gypsies pursuing must necessarily be very slow over all those obstacles. So I waited there watching the fallen masonry, the dark brown earth, the roots of trees clutching for moisture in the dim air, and fungoid growths that throve in the darkness; or, to be strictly accurate, as I should be when explaining this new invention, I sat at my table in the window here with the place-knob of the futuroscope turned exactly on that old tower, and the time-knob five or six centuries on. Lifting my pen to take notes of exactly what I saw, turned my eye from the futuroscope; and once more from my window, looking across the valley away to the southwest, I saw a white burst of smoke coming out of the hill, as another train ran to Dover. Turning back to the futuroscope I waited a long time peering down where shafts of sunlight illuminated the gloom, and never taking my eye off the heaps of masonry that lay at the end of the shaft. And at last I saw a shape, which I knew to be Kate, coming out of the dark of the tunnel into the dim light, clambering adroitly and strongly and without sign of fatigue over the obstacles lying where the railway track had run, and pushing deftly through veils of descending roots. She came into the direct light of the day, that streamed down that shaft through the brambles, and climbed deftly over the mouldering mosses of masonry and passed out of my sight.

Again came one of those despairs that have assailed me before. I wanted to cry out, even to hint to her, a warning that there awaited her at the end of the tunnel a creature as much savager than she as she was savager than the folk of our day. But there was no way of doing it. She went on, and I counted as well as I could every second after she had passed from my sight, to see what lead she had over the gypsies; and it was some while before any sign of their pursuit came to my notice. And then I heard faintly away to the north a bar of that tune that Lee played on his pipe. I was glad to hear him playing it, for it meant that the pursuit was not so rapid as it might have been had they been running, which he could not have been while playing a tune on a pipe. But Lee probably relied as much on the lure of his tune as he did upon speed, thinking perhaps that there was something irresistible in its strange melody. But it had not been so with Kate, for her flight was steady and purposeful. Still, the gypsies were not delaying, and sooner than I had expected I heard the tune quite near me, echoing through the tunnel as loud as Lee could play. And then the leading gypsy came in sight, and Lee close behind him, still playing, clambered over the great mounds of weeds and clay that clothed the fallen masonry and went on down the tunnel the way that Kate had gone, and four or five more of them followed, going over or round the obstacles as nimbly as foxhounds. Into the darkness of the ruined tunnel Lee's tune dwindled away, and all was still again where the faded daylight glimmered on weeds and heaps of dank clay and fungus. I stayed there watching a long time, but there was no more to see.

What would happen at the far end of the tunnel if there was still a way through? That was my next thought. And to that end Joe and his three sons were now on their way. So I switched the light over the hill and found them at once, and turned it straight on to them. The sheep were out on the hill in the sole charge of Toby. They left the sheep behind them and went on towards the end of the tunnel. So many orchids bloomed on the sunny slope over which they were walking, that it was clear to any observer that their race had survived the deadly snow with more ease than the race of Man. The petals of the wild roses lay on the grass and all the air was heavy with the sweet scent of the privet, and butterflies were now folding their wings to sleep on the stalks of dry grasses. How peaceful that valley seemed, and as though it were peaceful for ever. Yet just where they were going now with their bows and spears there had been a battle once, and Aelric, King of Kent, had been overthrown at Otford by Offa, King of Mercia, and 1261 years later the fate of nations had been decided all along that valley and many others, with blows whose circular scars on the faces of those calm hills I was still able to trace. And then perhaps a hundred years after that, shining all along this horizon, the great flash had come, the cause of which I have never quite understood, and I do not like to go back to that time with the futuroscope, because it was really too much for my eyesight; and after that the deadly snow had fallen which buried so much in this valley, a last white page that seems to have ended their history.

Now shadow was down over all that hill along which went the four armed men, for Bill considered himself a man now that he had been allowed to take part with his bow in this warlike expedition, and the sun was shining only upon the opposite hill, the stalks of whose grasses all dry in July were gleaming like fairy gold. And now the disk with which I watched them touched that end of the hill, through which I so often see the Dover train rush out with its burst of white smoke, and there to my astonishment I saw smoke again. I was not looking out of my window now, but through the futuroscope, and I was not only astonished but for some moments quite confused. Had a train strayed into this century in which even a cog was unknown? Or had the futuroscope gone suddenly wrong? Or had these changing centuries completely muddled my mind? And then I saw that what was muddling me seemed quite clear to the four armed men, from which I saw that the futuroscope must be working all right and that there was some sense in it after all. For they spread out and moved down to the southeast, and then turned and came up towards the mouth of the tunnel, from which the smoke was still rising. I turned the disk into the tunnel, and there in the dim light I saw the huge shape of the Wild Man, sitting beside his fire, the smoke of which went up to the roof and then slid outwards; and that was the smoke I had seen and not the smoke of the train, which was of course lying somewhere now covered with grass or moss, giving with its old iron a certain luxuriance to weeds.

I ran the disk further in, to look for Liza, who I knew must be in there, because the four men were going to rescue her and they would obviously know more about it than I did. But the skins that the Wild Man had hung up there on poles, and Nature's screen of clematis and her inner veils of the roots of trees and the smoke from fire, all made it too dark to see any more after I had gone in a little way. I say "after I had gone in" because I lived now so much with the futuroscope, and my interest had been so much caught up with the interest of that family, that I sometimes forget that I am sitting at a table in a window of a small house on a slope of the Darenth valley and that it is still the twentieth century. I ran the disk then further into the cavern past the huge shape of the Wild Man, looking no more civilized than Polyphemus, and found only darkness. The four men with their bows and spears were coming nearer and I felt confident that four to one, in spite of the Wild Man's hugeness, they would be able to rescue Liza. But what of Kate, of whom they knew nothing? Bert cannot have known of the gypsies' return from the island promontory, where Sydenham rose from the great London crater, and he must have pictured her still with her father in the hut beyond the horizon, where the slopes looked still on the sun, while the long shadows covered all the hill upon which Bert was standing. So, while the four approached the entrance to the cavern to rescue Liza, I ran the disk inside into the dark and listened. But I could hear no sound of the gypsies. The flute had stopped, and it was that that made me think the pursuit continued in earnest. I could have heard it a long way through that tunnel, but there was no sound, and I did not expect to hear any sound of the hide-clad feet. I listened carefully, but still none.

And then the Wild Man saw Joe and his sons approaching. He reached a long arm behind him and gathered his two great sticks. I ran the disk back and turned it full on him and saw him stand up and stride towards the daylight and stand there huge in the entrance to his cavern. The four men still came on. Then from inside the cavern for the first time I heard a faint sound. I moved the luminous disk back into the cavern at once, as far as any light strayed in. And there I saw Kate. How far she was ahead of the gypsies I could not tell, but none were in sight. The Wild Man was facing the other way, and all she had to do was to run past him and she would have found Bert. And she was about to do so. But at that moment there came a metallic clink from some bit of iron that the gypsies must have been carrying, which had hit against some fragment of fallen masonry. The Wild Man spun round at once, as a wild animal does the moment he hears metal. Anyone who has seen a wild animal hearing the clink of metal will know what I mean; anyone who has not can try it, and he will know the instantaneous suddenness with which that wild man turned. To the wild beast the clink of metal warns of Man at once. To the Wild Man it must have told of an age he had never known, an age of which those hereditary guardians, his instincts, warned him, an age that only metal could bring back. How much of that age his dim intuitions told him I cannot say: that is the work of the novelist. I only saw the flashing turn of that huge bulk and an urgency in his face and his whole attitude as that one clink of metal warned him of what I cannot guess. He turned as an escaped slave might turn who hears the clink of his old chain. But what did he really fear? If those instincts that warned him spoke true, calling out of old ages that his forbears had known, there was no question of chains; it was not chains that metal would bring to him. It was a white collar, a white starched collar fastened with a stud, which had enslaved his ancestors for generations. That would be too strong a word to use; but there had been no escape from it. Without that white collar they would have been outcasts. Now he was free; the age of iron was gone. What did that clink of metal on fallen brick tell to his instincts? I cannot tell; for we do not know how far instincts and intuitions range, nor what knowledge they have, nor how much of it they bring home to the hearts from which they started. Perhaps he saw a shop in Hastings again and felt with some ancestral feeling, awakened by the clink of that gypsy's iron, the pinch on some forbear's neck of starch and a collar-stud. Inland a little way, at Wilmington, stood an older ancestor's portrait. I thought, as he spun round swiftly, he would be free like him.

Chapter XXV

Just as the Wild Man heard the clink of metal and turned round, as a tiger turns at the sound of a rifle touching a rock, to fight against an enemy of his entire era, Kate had the daylight before her and Bert standing there, and was free. Just for that moment she was free, and then she saw the Wild Man rushing towards her with one of his great clubs raised, and she turned and fled, and fled in the wrong direction, straight back to the gypsies. I only caught a glimpse of her as she turned; then the dark of the tunnel hid her, and the Wild Man rushing behind her, infuriated by the clink of iron which threatened his way of life. Then I saw Joe and his three sons advance into the cavern, and there were three ages now in that tunnel, the Neolithic age, in which Joe and his family dwelt, the Paleolithic age, in which Man first used stone, and back into which the man with the two great sticks had strayed, and the dawn of the iron age, which had overthrown the two ages of stone, and through which the gypsies were wandering. So they will always wander through any age, a bright patch of colour and a murmur of song, in many lands but of none. In the tunnel I could only hear sounds, but could make out nothing from them, and they grew fainter and fainter and soon I heard them no more, as Joe and his three sons went into the dimness and were nearly lost to my sight. But while I could distinguish them still Liza came out to meet them from a little hollow in one of the walls, curtained with deerskins.

"Liza!" they all shouted.

The object of their quest was fulfilled. Bert knew nothing of Kate. He had not seen her when I saw her, just at the edge of the daylight, and she had not seen Bert when she turned and fled. A few seconds more and they would have come together, but those seconds were not to be had. Time out of his great wealth of centuries had not granted them. But at this moment Liza was free; her father and brothers had rescued her. Yet she did not run towards them as Kate had been running, but took a few steps slowly, as though to receive them. She said nothing, and in wonder at her silence they did not speak either. I looked carefully at her face, but could not make out what she thought. And then her father spoke.

"We have rescued you," he said.

She smiled.

"We have come to bring you home," he said.

She smiled a little again, and walked towards them and went with them to the mouth of the tunnel. But there she stopped, and smiled at them again. I turned the light full on their faces, and there I saw dawn on all of them, slowly, and even on Bill, the realization that Liza was seeing them off. She was the hostess of that dark cavern, her rescuers were visitors whom she was pleased to see, but to whom now she was saying farewell. In the faces of the four who would have rescued her I saw only astonishment. I looked at her face again, narrowing the luminous disk till I saw nothing else, and I tried to puzzle it out. She stood, as it seemed to me, between the workaday world, as she thought it, and what to her may even have been civilization, and on the other hand what was wild and strange and to her may have seemed romantic. And she had chosen romance. I turned the light to look at her father and brothers, and they were standing there still. I saw a look of horror come over her father's face. She was untrue to the neolithic age! I looked at Liza again, and her eyes seemed to be gazing away to some dream that to her was romance, away from the accustomed, from the humdrum, as she may have thought it, towards wildness, towards some savage ideal that our race had once and which they have long lost, and which among the eddies and currents of time seemed to have reappeared where the rails of the Southeastern railway were rusting away and making less mark in the grass than the work of the mole.

There was no argument. I do not think talk came so easily to those people as it does to us. But I think their intuitions may have been quicker, and they saw how it was sooner than I did and silently turned away. Liza picked up a log, a log I could hardly have lifted, and threw it on the fire and turned back to the tunnel and, parting two skins that hung from a pole on the wall, she went under an arch of brickwork into the ruins of one of those hollows that railway companies provide here and there in their tunnels. Her action in following the will-o'-the-wisp of romance, backwards to that dark age she appeared to have chosen, seemed strange to me, and to everybody but me will seem still stranger; but it must be remembered what I have seen, even if I do not quite know what it was; but, whatever it was, our age goes forward to it, to the flash that I saw and the deadly snow and the great London crater. Liza went backwards.

I followed the four as they went dejectedly over the slope while pigeons flew homewards and the sunlight left the eastern slope of the valley where the grass had shone all gold, and went to the tops of the trees and then went even from them, and colour went from the earth and into the sky. Bert spoke first.

"I can go and see Kate now," he said to his father.

"Yes," said Joe.

They went on in silence again. They entered the hut and Maud looked at them and seemed to know how it was.

"She won't come?" she said.

Joe shook his head. No-one said anything more. I saw that Bert was not planning to go over the hill that night.

There was nothing more for me to do there, and I could see nothing in the dark of the tunnel. So I disconnected the futuroscope and had my supper.

I was puzzled a good deal that evening over Liza's queer point of view. She certainly had not much civilization in her home; but what she had she was deserting just for the lure of something wild and strange. I saw what she might have argued, had I been able to argue with her, and I saw my own answers to all that she could have said. And then it occurred to me that she would not have argued at all, but only relied on her intuitions and instincts; and that those are usually right. So what could my logic avail, even if it had been possible to talk things over with her? At this thought I gave it up, as I have had to give up so many perplexing theories that I might have worked out if they had been confined to one century, but mixing ideas of our time with those of five hundred years hence is very confusing, and all the more so when the ideas of those people whom I was watching are not original, but seem to be mostly derived from those other ages of which I know so little except their names, the neolithic and the paleolithic.

From this I turned to a thought that more nearly concerns me: what is the legal definition of a futuroscope? I might define it in one way, but the law might define it in another, and then the man from the Post Office might define it in yet another, through being quite ignorant of what it really is. And who could blame him? So the question that troubled me for the rest of the evening was, would I have to pay a licence for the futuroscope? And how could I explain the difference between it and a television set, which is not so very apparent? And how could I prove that that difference existed, to a man who had never seen a futuroscope before, or an official in London who had not even seen this one? In the end, little though I can afford it, I decided to pay the licence whenever requested to do so, and so purchase immunity from all the worry of making out a case to the contrary. And by then it was time to go to bed.

I got up early next morning, because I was quite sure that Bert would start as soon as it was light. It was a lovely summer's morning, and I may mention here that I have always found it a distinct convenience to keep the time-knob of a futuroscope not only at the same time of day but at the same time of year as it is in the century that one is looking at. Thus the change of century is less jarring then it would be if it went in a moment, as one does with the futuroscope, from, say, 6 in the evening in December to noon in midsummer. One can very easily make such changes, but the owner of one of these instruments will feel less lost among the centuries if he goes from here to there at the same time of day and the same time of year. So very early on that July morning, with larks rising up from meadows to sing in the pale-blue sky, I went into an early July morning of five or six centuries on and, with my eye hovering over the Darenth valley, I saw, just as I had expected, a solitary figure with spear and bow moving up the grassy slope on the western side before the woods were awake. It was Bert on his way to see Kate, and I could tell from his easy stride that, though he went armed as a precaution against wolves, he had no idea that Kate was not in perfect safety in her father's house still asleep.

As I followed him through the wood all the birds were waking, and rabbits were slipping out of its shadows to feed on the grass below. Down one of the glades as we went I heard the rolling thunder of hooves, and knew from the sound that a herd of horses had woken and was galloping free in that bright morning air. And then I got a glimpse of their manes flowing wildly from their curved necks, and their splendid tails streaming like comets, not only in shape, but they flashed in the sunlight too. So they too, like man, and so many other creatures and all the wild flowers, had survived that flash that I saw and the deadly snow. No butterflies were yet abroad, but all those flowers that sleep when we do were waking and the trees were full of song. All this much I could see, but something in Bert's eyes showed me that he saw them with greater intensity, as he strode on through the wood with happiness in his face, not knowing the disappointment that was awaiting him. Out of the wood he entered a burst of sunlight bathing the far slope with gold, up which the long shadows were already retreating, and far before him the waters of the great London crater shone in the morning. He walked down joyously towards the old archer's hut, till we could hear the whistle of flocks of widgeon and teal that were dancing in the air of the bright morning in intricate curves between the lake and the sky. Then something about the reed-thatched hut of the archer, or its little garden, seemed desolate to Bert. I saw that in his face, though I don't know what it was that he noticed. At that look I turned the disk of the futuroscope from him and ran it on ahead and into the hut. And sure enough only Bob was there, asleep on a bed of reeds. Sooner than I had expected Bert was into the hut, and his entry woke the old man at once, who sat up rustling on his reedy bed.

"Where's Kate?" said Bert.

"Gone," said the old man.

Those people never used many words.

"With the gypsies?" asked Bert.

And the old men nodded his head.

Bert stood in thought for a moment, then walked out of the hut and the old man jumped up and followed him. I brought the disk of the futuroscope out into the open air and looked all round to see what I could see, but there was no sign of the gypsies; only the golden morning full of the birds and beasts undisturbed by man, which seemed to have come back to the glories of morning, the mystery of the woods and the wide gleam of the sky, now that Man was nearly gone, as Adam and Eve might have found on one happy day, had it not been forbidden, that the angel had sheathed his flaming sword and departed. For a moment the beauty of the morning lured my interest away from Bert's troubles, as he and Kate's father stood by the door perplexed. Like a child resting his elbows dreamily on a windowsill and gazing out at the morning, a hawk rested far above them on the still air. Then I ran the light towards Knockbolt at the northern end of the tunnel, and just as I left them I saw that they were setting off in the same direction. I got to the end of the tunnel with a single twist of my finger, and the bright valley shining beside it was silent and empty. I ran back the disk to Bob and Bert and saw Bob talking and pointing before I heard what he said, and he was evidently telling of what I had already seen outside that end of the tunnel. What went on in the middle of the tunnel neither he nor I knew. But it seemed clear enough that whatever fight there had been between the Wild Man and the gypsies, and whoever had won, Kate had foolishly run right into the gypsies and been carried off by them. The gypsies had retreated out of the tunnel, as Bob was now explaining to Bert, and had gone away with Kate and he had been unable to save her. I saw Bert impatient and urging the old man to say where the gypsies had gone, and at first he could only point. And every time he pointed Bert's face grew graver, and I saw an apprehension growing upon it though I did not know of what. They went up to the top of the tunnel, and the old man pointed again southeastwards over the woods, and I heard Bert cry out suddenly, "To the Old Stones!"

Chapter XXVI

I knew nothing of the rites of these people whom I had been watching for so long, now, but I saw from the horror with which Bert had gasped "The Old Stones!" that this circle of monoliths at Coldrum, to which the old man had pointed, so old today that a few more centuries had probably stroked their outlines only a little smoother, were evidently the scene of some rites in this far future, of which I knew nothing, as they had been in the far past. I left the old archer pointing and Bert staring, and ran the disk of the futuroscope the way they were looking, out of the chalk country, till I came to the sand where the bracken grew; and sure enough the old man's line led straight to Coldrum, and I had not cast about for more than a minute or so before I found the old circle of twenty-four stones, lying amongst the grass like hippopotami resting, and about eighteen more of them fallen down the slope of the little hill on which the circle had stood. Then I ran the bright disk back to see if that was where the gypsies were going. And they were. I came on them in a sort of lane through the forest, heading straight in the direction in which the old archer had pointed. I looked close and saw Kate was among them, walking and apparently free, but never unwatched. I could not think what Bert and Kate's father could do. They were only two against a tribe. I ran back the light to them to hear if they planned anything, and turned it full on them to see what hope they had. They were going forward where the old man had pointed, and they soon come to the forest. There I saw them pick up a trail that was scarcely a path, far less a road, but there was just room for a cart on it in and out among the great beech-trees. It was a grassy ride in which I could see no tracks, but they evidently satisfied themselves that the gypsies had gone that way.

They walked in silence over the sand which cloaks the top of the hill, till the slope ran downward before them and they came to the chalk, where the bracken ceased suddenly and different flowers grew. And on that slope they came to a clearing where three great trees had been cut and taken away by I know not whom, and the sunlight streamed in and, looking out from the bright space, the two men stopped and saw the chalk valleys rolling and rippling away, and beyond them wide to the skyline the view of the Weald. I listened to hear what they would say; but neither of them spoke and they only gazed. And then Bert evidently saw what he sought, some moving specks in the Weald, which I could not see, and he pointed them out to the archer, who could not see them either. But it was the gypsies going towards the Old Stones. I could see that they had not any doubt of that. The Weald like a great sea into which the vales of the wold ran down like rivers was mostly forest, and the three or four plumes of smoke rising up in the morning out of all that wide view showed how rare were members of the human species, which had once so crowded the world. Birds sang happily enough five or six centuries earlier, that is before I turned on the futuroscope twenty minutes ago, but they seemed to be singing ever more happily now. That of course must have been my imagination, for they cannot really feel like that about Man. Still Bert and Kate's father stood silent, gazing over the Weald, and still I listened to hear what they would plan; for I could think, myself, of nothing that they could do to rescue her from that band. They certainly would not let Bert play again the trick that had succeeded so well once. And yet Bert when he spoke could think of nothing better.

"They are going to the Old Stones," he said with a troubled note in his voice.

And the old man nodded his head.

"Will they camp for the night?" asked Bert.

"Yes," said Kate's father, and he spoke as though he knew the gypsies' ways and was quite sure of that.

And I could see that Bert was satisfied that he knew.

"We must go into their encampment by night," he said.

The old archer did not answer, but stayed gazing over the Weald.

"We will take our bows and go in from opposite sides," said Bert.

"No," said the old archer, "I have a better plan than that."

The gypsies were probably about five miles ahead, though I could not make them out, even though a light mist that lay over the Weald was lifting as we watched, to be driven away by the morning. The futuroscope gave me a wonderful view, though the young eyes of Bert, unspoiled by civilization, must have had a far clearer one, while clearest of all was the view of a hawk resting in the blue sky. And now, as Bert turned his eyes away from the Weald to speak to Bob, I could see that the gypsies must have passed out of his sight under the oaks again. But he was satisfied that they were going where he dreaded, though what he dreaded I did not know. Coldrum is a place of ancient rites of which we know nothing, and it seemed to me that rites were performed there again of which I was just as ignorant. A hill beside it on which no holly grows is called Holly Hill, and it is thought that Holly is certainly a corruption of holy; and it is altogether a mysterious place.

"What would you do?" asked Bert.

"You must run," said the old man, "and get to Canterbury by evening and get the Seer of Canterbury to come to the Old Stones. He will do it if you tell him it is to thwart the gypsies, for they have altered the shape of iron."

"Can he save Kate?" asked Bert.

"He can keep them away from the Old Stones," said Bob.

"How?" said Bert.

"By arriving there before them," said Bob. "You must get him to travel during some of the night. They will not leave their camp till after dawn. Then when he is there let him send a messenger bidding all men come to the Circle, because he requires an offering. And the gypsies will know that he will take one of them, because of what they did to iron, and they will keep away from the Old Stones until he has made his offering."

Bert stood silent, thinking over the plan.

"Quick," said Bob. And Bert started away towards Canterbury, which lies beyond the Old Stones, walking, I should say, a steady six miles an hour.

So that is what they did again at Coldrum. I say *again* because the only time I ever saw it, actually walking there, I noticed that one of the great stones had been hollowed to make what looked like a rather shallow bath, and I had wondered at the time if it was for blood. And then the hill near it being called Holy Hill, if that was the right interpretation of it, was enough to show that the place was religious; and there have been very few religions on earth that have never had the terrible belief that God would be pleased by their killing something, always human once, and then in later ages cattle or sheep. And the words of the old archer taught me that they were doing it again at Coldrum. Now that Bert was gone away to the Weald the old archer stood there uncertain, and I watched him till he walked slowly away, going in the direction of the gypsies. I could not help him, I could not help Kate, I could not do anything at all in that far future; so I turned to my own affairs and switched off the futuroscope and, as it were, came home.

It may seem from my frequent descriptions of what these people were doing, or perhaps I should say what they will do, while of myself I only tell of turning the futuroscope on and off, that they have far more to do than I. But this is by no means the case. I have, for instance, to consult the bills of the Electricity Board, and to attempt to understand them even if I do not quite know exactly what watts are, and then to pay them, and to attend to several other things; and the only reason I do not mention them is because they are so uninteresting, not because I am idle. To such things as these I attended for the rest of the day, except for a quick look away to the south about suppertime, to see if the gypsies were camping, as Kate's father had said they would do. And sure enough, they were. I found them where three or four huge oaks had elbowed lesser trees away and were lifting their magnificent limbs over smooth swards. The gypsies had travelled idly and had come no more than half way from the flowery valley, that was once cut for the railway to the circle of stones that were placed there for unknown rites. The hooded cart was there with the horse unhitched, and a fire was burning and the gypsy children were playing all through the glades, and Kate was walking about, but never far from the fire and the cart, and I noticed that all the gypsy men were well away from the little encampment at various points all round, where I found it hard to pick them up behind the great oaks, and they were evidently making sure that nobody would approach their camp unseen again.

I was very glad to see that the old archer was right and that the gypsies were camping there. For, whatever they were going to do to Kate at the Old Stones, the rest for the night would give Bert and the Seer time to come from Canterbury and get to Coldrum before the gypsies. There was nothing more that I could do; indeed, I had done nothing at all. I am merely introducing the futuroscope to the public and trying to explain a few of the pleasures to be derived from it; and, however much my interest may have got tangled up with the fortunes of this rather primitive family, I could do nothing more for them. Had I been offering the story of any family and its little romances, I should certainly have chosen one whose civilization and culture were more worthy of my reader's attention; but the purpose of these notes was merely to keep in line with modern inventions and to explain some of the details of this one and its potentialities to the public. And in the course of writing these notes I have allowed my interest to be lured away in the unfortunate manner that my reader will have noticed by now. I can only go on with my story of Bert and Kate, and my odd account of Liza, and hope that even though I tell of so simple a people, I may nevertheless have something of some slight interest to show of how a futuroscope works.

Well, then, I switched off the futuroscope after my supper and gave no more attention to it that night; but I got up quite early next morning and connected up the futuroscope, and the luminous disk lay on the grass under the oak-trees in the forest of the Weald where I had left it. The gypsies were gone, but only just gone, for their fires were still smouldering, and little wisps of smoke were straggling up through the handfuls of earth they had thrown on them. So I had not far to turn the knob before I overtook them, and there they were with their hooded cart rambling along the primitive lane under the great trees, still heading towards Coldrum. In front of them playing a merry tune on his pipe went Lee, and I was relieved to see his sprightly step and to hear his merry tune, for they somehow showed me at once that it was at any rate not to sacrifice Kate with some old barbarous rite that they went toward the Old Stones. But if not sacrifice, what then? It was pretty clear to me that Kate was to be married against her will in that grim circle that to them was holy, and obviously to Lee. Would Bert and the Seer of Canterbury arrive in time?

Now, here is one of the advantages of the futuroscope; and much though I have allowed my sympathies to stray away from any scientific purpose, I can at least explain this: I could see with a mere flick of the finger what was happening at the same moment many miles away. I ran the luminous disk as far as the Old Stones, roughly estimating the distance as I went, which I put at about eight miles, and then I ran it towards Canterbury, hunting about in the forest among the few tracks that there were, till at length I picked up Bert, and the Seer of Canterbury was with him, holding his long staff. They were rather further from Coldrum than the gypsies were, but walking a steady pace, while the gypsies rambled and only went the pace of their children, who, though they could mostly run nearly as fast as rabbits, were always chasing butterflies or foxes or squirrels when they were moving their fastest, and made no faster progress in the gypsies' direction than a child of today would make when taking a walk with its nurse. Backwards and forwards I ran the luminous disk to see how Bert and Lee were getting on, and I must have spent nearly an hour doing this, till I satisfied myself that the two of them were now about the same distance from the Old Stones, which was about five or six miles. After that I watched only the gypsies. They could have easily got to Coldrum before the Seer of Canterbury, had the men gone on ahead of the pony; but I saw that they meant all to keep together for the rite at the Old Stones, and the pony's pace was only a third of that of Bert's, or, now that his pace was that of the Seer of Canterbury, about half.

Sometimes I ran my luminous disk away from the gypsies over the forest through which they wandered, and looked at the butterflies and birds and badgers and squirrels as I have never looked at them before. It is really wonderful to be in a forest, divested of the terror that is so natural to Man. Though knowing this terror existed, one had given it little more notice than a fox does to his smell, but when it was gone the effect of its loss was amazing. Never have I seen even butterflies quite so close, and I was astonished at the beauty of their intricate designs, which showed in the sunlight as it never does when they are dead. I saw the grey and white fur of a badger as he went to his sandy home away from the light of day, and it came to me with surprise that in all my life I had never seen one before. And then squirrels, if I went for a walk in a wood, always seemed to be on the far side of the trunk of a tree; I could hear their claws scratching and their derisive laugh, but they were hardly ever on the same side as I was. Stoats I saw too, with their powerful shoulders, hunting, and sometimes lizards, and several rarer animals, though most of the ones I saw were rare to me. And sometimes I saw stalking through the trees one whose ancestor in our day is pussy, but who looked then more like a small tiger. But an opportunity unrolled itself before me for a whole volume on natural history, another opportunity wasted, for I have not the qualification for it, and my interest is lured away to that wild creature Kate and her barbarous young man Bert, both of whom had slipped in five or six centuries from the peaks of our civilization all the way back to the age that we know as the Neolithic.

Chapter XXVII

Much of that morning I spent watching the gypsies' progress, and then that of Bert and the Seer, and then the gypsies again. It was pleasant to loiter through that lovely forest, unspoiled for five hundred years, and I thought all was going well, Bert and the Seer having already a lead over the gypsies, which with their better pace was all that one wanted. And then, as I drifted the disk over the forest back from the gypsies to them, I suddenly saw them hurry away to their right. Bert had evidently caught some glimpse of the gypsies in a glade of the forest, or more likely among those great oaks he could not have seen them, but saw birds flying away and knew it must be from the gypsies. He hurried and was urging the Seer of Canterbury to hurry as much as he could. I could not understand that manoeuvre, for turning away like that to the north was just what would give the gypsies a chance of arriving first at the Old Stones for their rite, which I felt sure was to be the marriage of Kate to Lee. The gypsies were coming from the southwest. I could not make it out, and I followed them closely with the luminous disk to see if I could get any clue. And then a word of Bert's that I chanced to hear explained everything. "We must come in from the other side," he said. "They daren't kill you in the stone circle."

And then I understood. Among so much that was before the iron age, and which came back when machinery was gone (since something had to take its place and the old things were waiting) was the sanctity, the mystery and the power of the old circle of stones. Then Parliament went, and the Post Office and the railways and roads, and in fact everything that dominates our civilization, the power of the Old Stones returned, and their rites were evidently binding on all. I saw Bert stooping behind every bit of cover, and hurrying and urging his companion to hurry, and I had no doubt that he feared death at the hand of the gypsies for both of them if the gypsies saw them before they got to the Old Stones. But once inside that circle I saw that the Seer was sacred, and that the rites within that grey circle were his and not to be challenged by anyone. The young gypsy men, had they seen them, could easily have run and caught the Seer and Bert before they reached the sacred stones. As I saw them running I ran the luminous disk back, to see if Bert and the Seer had been noticed. But they had not, and the forest was so thick there that Bert could certainly only have known of the gypsies' presence by the birds that they were disturbing. They went on slowly still, with Lee piping in front, the children running in and out of the trees, and the gypsy women adding a touch of colour to the sunlight with the bright scarves in their hair and their ear-rings of gold flashing. Now they and the other two would reach opposite sides, and the race was a far closer thing than what I had thought it would be. Just as the Seer would be sacred if he reached the sanctuary of the stones, so the marriage of Kate would be valid if the gypsies got there first; for the rites of the Old Stones appeared to be everything. How the sanctity of those old grey stones had come down the ages I do not know; but it seemed to have remained dormant for a few thousand years, as though the old stones had slept lying there in the grass and had now woken again.

As the gypsies strolled through the forest I looked at Kate walking with them, with Mrs. Smith near her and watching, and I saw from a frightened look on her face as she looked at the line of hills under which lay the Old Stones that she knew the power of that mysterious circle. For the tops of those low hills were now visible through occasional spaces among the boughs of the oaks, and they were on the far side of the Stones. I turned back to Bert and the Seer and they were still hurrying away rather on the arc of a circle and getting no nearer the Stones, and I knew there would be no safety for them if the gypsies got to the circle and found them outside. The Seer moved like a fugitive, not like the great magician he would be if he could get to the ancient circle. Still Bert was hurrying him on. I turned back to the gypsies, and still they were strolling slowly and the look of fear was now settled down on Kate's face. The gypsies knew of no need to hurry, and it sometimes seemed that there was none, and that even at that slow pace their leaders might reach the ancient circle first. I ran the light back to Bert and the Seer of Canterbury to see what the chances were, and they seemed about even. I did this again and again, but I could not be sure how the strange race was going, because Bert and the Seer had not yet reached the point from which they intended to come in from the opposite side from the gypsies, with the bare hills behind them and the forest in front. Soon Lee's wild tune would be audible to them in the stillness of that summer's morning, warning them to hurry still more; but they would still be unseen by the gypsies, for the hillock the Old Stones crowned was now between them and the gypsies, and they could not be seen any more from the other side till they reached the Stones themselves. The bracken grew on deep sand all round the gypsies, gold sand that grew the great oaks and made warm homes for the badgers and which had once been useful to men, as I saw from a green scar here and there which had once clearly been quarries.

The gypsies were very near now and the frightened look on Kate's face was very clear. But Bert and the Seer had reached at last the point from which they turned and went straight for the Old Stones, hurrying, and when they were only about three hundred yards away they were the same distance from the circle of stones as the leading gypsies were. Not till then did my uneasiness cease, and I had no longer any doubt that Bert and the Seer would win. In two minutes they were there, and the Seer stood up in the front of the circle, and the gypsies were still a hundred and fifty yards away. The front of the circle was on the very edge of the steep mound, and was quite different from all the rest of the circle. Over the edge of the mound, where it was steepest, vandalism or time, or those two ill-assorted companions working together, had pushed about eighteen of the stones, which now lay fallen at the bottom of the slope. But one cluster of great stones stood together there at the very edge, making something like three sides of a paved square, the fourth side being open to the dawn where it would appear on midsummer's day, and there the Seer stood, facing the east, and the gypsies saw him as they approached the Stones. And Bert called out a welcome and the Seer smiled towards them and all the gypsies stopped. And Bert waved to them to come forward and called out, "It is the Seer. He needs an offering."

They had come to the edge of the forest, but not all of them had quite left the shelter of the oaks and some ancient apple trees, which must have been once an orchard, that stood at the edge. And suddenly there were no gypsies in sight at all. I never saw anyone vanish more quickly. Only their cart stood there; and then someone turned even that round, and they were all gone and Kate with them. Kate was now safe from the rite among the Old Stones, but she was still a prisoner. I did not follow them, for I knew that they were gone to the gypsies' home, which is the forest and the road, and that they would not dare to come near the Old Stones while the Seer was there, and what would happen after that I could not guess. So I moved the disk over all the Old Stones instead, and examined their queer circle. Meanwhile Bert brought bread and cheese from a wallet, and he and the Seer sat down to eat after their long walk; but I noticed they did not do so until they had moved outside the circle of sacred stones. Then I examined the stones at my leisure. I looked again at the one that was slightly hollowed, but had no way of telling whether it was hollowed for blood or for what, or even whether it had been hollowed for certain by man or by time. Then I looked at the small roofless room that was made by four great slabs and was open towards the east. There the Seer had stood, and there I had no doubt he greeted the rising sun when it looked in on the rites, slightly squinting at them now, though once he had looked at them full face in the days of the earlier people who had built that altar facing the dawn, not knowing that the dawn would ever shift from its place, or that any of the great stones would fall, or their rites be forgotten awhile, as we do not know what of ours will pass away.

Chapter XXVIII

I stood there in the circle of standing and fallen stones, invisible beside Bert and the Seer of Canterbury, wondering what could be done to save Kate, and seeing nothing. When I say I stood, I am making a mistake: I sat at my table in the window, looking into the futuroscope at which I have spent so much time during the last few weeks, so much time that the world of six hundred years hence, the world of forests over our fields and cities, is somewhat more real to me now than the world of trains and motors and news and taxes in which I suppose I am really living. But all my interests are slipping away and are now six centuries hence, concerning themselves with the fate of people whose barbarism is, sometimes I almost feel, an insult to my reader, to whom I should like to offer information of scientific value or studies of far more sociological importance than what I have offered, if only I were qualified to deal with such matters and had not been led away by my anxieties about these little lesser things. How then, I wondered, was it possible for them to rescue Kate? They had saved her from any ceremony at the Old Stones; but how could they get her home, either to her father's house or to the reed-built home of which she and Bert dreamed. Bert and the Seer were gazing, undecided, and I did not hear them speak and I turned again to look at the Old Stones; and, as I looked at the fallen monsters lying at the bottom of the slope on which the rest of the circle stood, I suddenly saw to my astonishment the last thing that I expected to see on such monuments that had strayed into the far future. I saw a large grey sheet of unmistakable metal firmly fixed to the stone.

I stared at it in astonishment; for, standing by those Old Stones so far in the future, as I seemed to be doing, I had forgotten the ages that came between the neolithic age and the one in which the Seer of Canterbury was standing beside Bert, and the one in which of course I am sitting now in my chair in a window overlooking the Darenth valley, but I had forgotten that. I narrowed the disk and looked closely at that old stone clasping its metal slab, and I saw that the slab was covered with writing, writing not engraved, but made by metal letters standing out from the plaque. Grass waved over the stone, but a slight wind was blowing, and by waiting long enough till blades of grass were blown clear from each letter in turn I was able to read the whole inscription. This is what it said: The Coldrum Stone Circle has been vested in the National Trust as a memorial to Benjamin Harrison 1837–1921 of Ightham, 10th January 1926.

So it had been there about six hundred years, and I was still able to read it, and think I have done so accurately. Time had not harmed that inscription, for they had used some unrusting metal, and it had survived whatever had wrecked the world we know, and the people of that far future had evidently not dared to touch it, because it was metal, and metal was to them an accursed thing, from which they felt that harm could come, though they knew not what. Curiously enough I found nothing inappropriate in that metal among those old stones, the English writing staring into the years that had forgotten the art of reading. For Benjamin Harrison was a link between the age of those old stones and ours. I knew the old man, having met him once when he came for a day to London, and his thoughts were all with those old ages of stone, as mine were being lured more and more every day, by the strange instrument that I had borrowed, into this Stone Age that had come back again and which had so easily taken control of the earth as though it were what was intended, returning after the interlude of a regime that had trusted to metal and had all gone away with the machines that had brought disaster.

I turned back to the Seer and Bert, who were still standing silent. If they had said anything while I was looking at the fallen stones, it was only to say that there was nothing to be done, for they had clearly made no plans. And as I watched them the Seer turned to Bert with one word that was evidently a leavetaking, and Bert bowed his head and the Seer went down the mound and away to the east on what must have been his long walk back to Canterbury. The sun, as I saw him go, flashed on a bright flint knife which hung from his belt, sharp and a little curved as if to fit a throat, and an odd fancy of mine in that wild scene made me imagine it had a thirsty look. Soon he turned and looked back to Bert and raised his right arm in what must have been some form of blessing that was given in that far time, and Bert bowed his head. And then he stood there disconsolate, as if left without any guidance. He did not move, but remained staring eastwards until forest hid the Seer. Still he stood motionless and I was about to turn the light off him, being depressed with his despair, when I saw a figure coming out of the forest from some oaks among which the gypsies had disappeared, but it was not one of the gypsies. He was coming straight for the Old Stones, and when he came near enough for me to recognize him I saw it was Bob, holding his great yew bow. Bert greeted him listlessly when he recognized him too, and I think the old archer saw that Bert despaired and did not seem to share his despair. Bert saw that the old man had come from watching the gypsies and must have known that he had seen Kate; but he showed no signs of hope arising from that. And then the old archer spoke.

"All the gypsy men are around Kate in the forest," he said, "and many of the women too."

And that brought no more reply from Bert than a nod of his head.

"And Mrs. Smith is unguarded, and often alone."

Bert said some word that I did not understand, but which sounded like some curse that they used in that distant age.

"We cannot rescue Kate," said the old archer.

And Bert wearily shook his head.

"But we can take away Mrs. Smith," said Bob.

Bert did not seem to think very quickly, and then a light dawned in his face.

"She is their queen bee," said the old archer, "their prophetess and their witch. Go back to the Darn."

That is what he called the Darenth and it struck me as odd, because the old men about here remember their grandfathers and grandmothers always calling the Darenth the Darn, and I suppose that human tongues coming on the same obstacle slid over it in the same way six centuries hence, when that tongue is no longer bitted and bridled by reading and writing which tend to make it pronounce every letter.

"Get your father and brothers," the old man went on, "and we will find their encampment by night. I know the way they have gone. When you have Mrs. Smith you may demand anything of them."

Bert wasted no time in making up his mind when once he had seen a way, and he turned from the mound at once and began walking towards his home, and Bob walked with him.

I had started early and had had an early breakfast, and now with a twist of my hand I roved about twelve miles and six hundred years and came home to attend to my own affairs which, trivial though they may be, are yet specks and atoms of a civilization incomparably higher than anything attained by the people I am writing about, unless it be that they, nearer to the knees of Mother Earth, are playing more as her children are meant to play, while we straying further away from them every few years are in danger of being lost. But these are speculations for philosophers, sociologists and scientists, and all manner of men that I am not.

I allowed them two or three hours to walk the distance to the hut beside what they called the Darn, and I had my lunch before they had theirs and did not turn on the futuroscope any more until the time that by my calculations Kate's father and Bert and the whole of their family would be well on their way after the gypsies. I had an early tea and then connected the futuroscope up again with the mains and turned the light on the Darenth, and found, as I had expected, that they had all started, with Maud all alone making cheese, and Toby looking after the sheep. Then I ran the light up the valley to find them, and greatly astonished I was when I did. And I may take this opportunity of warning all users of the futuroscope to look out for astonishments; for we not only have our own ideas of what the future will be, but we have a great many opinions in writing to guide us and, indeed, get indications every day about what is going to happen, and even direct prophecies; and, when one finds the future so different from all that, the difference is likely to jar. And so users of a futuroscope should be prepared for surprises at all times. It is not like television, where the programme has all been prepared in accordance with most of our tastes, so that one knows what to expect.

The surprise that I met on that afternoon was a minor one, but still it was a surprise, and, as I picked up Joe and his sons and Bob, I saw the huge form of the Wild Man with them, walking along with his two great sticks. I can only suppose that Liza had heard from Maud about what the gypsies were doing with Kate, and that she had persuaded her Wild Man to go and help. But one cannot always say what influence a woman exerts, and I do not know what had happened, except that I saw the Wild Man there, walking along with the rest towards the forest into which the gypsies had gone, an alliance of the paleolithic and neolithic ages against the age that had overthrown both, the age of the very first appearance of metal, that is usually known as the Bronze Age. It was strange to see these two old ages coming into their own again, while the Bronze Age seemed to stray through the country like a stranger. I kept the luminous disk on them, and noticed as they went up the valley that opened into the Weald that nothing seemed to regard them as intruders or strangers, and, walking beside them, as I seemed to be doing, I came nearer to rabbits and hares than I had ever been before. What language the Wild Man spoke I did not know, for he was not speaking to any of them, but walked along beside them, though a little bit wide, like a dog joining in with others because they are having a hunt. Bob was leading and seemed sure of the way, and so they came to the forest. But they still had a long way to go, and after a while I began to think of my supper, not because it could compare in importance with plans to rescue a girl who had been barbarously stolen, but because I knew that they could not come up with the gypsies before sunset and did not expect them to do anything until nightfall.

So, after carefully noting their direction and leaving the place-knob just where it was, I disconnected the futuroscope and sat down to my supper, wondering all the time what was to happen to Kate and whether this small armed band would succeed in capturing the arch-witch of the gypsies and whether the capture of her would be such a blow to them that they would give up Kate. After supper I read the paper, for I realized, as of late I have sometimes found it difficult to realize, that I am still living in the twentieth century and must, like everybody else, have some idea of how it is getting on. So much that I read would have been shocking to the people whose lives I had been watching for so long, for people seldom tolerate what they cannot easily understand, and I fear that to all other readers of those papers the people of whom I tell will seem very ignorant and even wrong-minded. They were human of course; but we are interested today in so many things besides mere humanity, and having seen what I suppose is the greatest triumph of the power and might of our scientists, I know that I shall be blamed for saying no more about it than that I saw a flash along the horizon and a fall of snow in July. But the truth is that it was too much for my eyesight, and I am definitely reluctant to turn the time-knob of my borrowed futuroscope back to examine the origin of that flash more closely. And so I tell instead of that very backward people, for whose simplicity I apologize.

Chapter XXIX

It was not till late that night that I connected up the futuroscope again. I had been waiting for it to get quite dark, not only here but over the forest of the Weald, into which Joe and his sons and Kate's father and the Wild Man were going about six hundred years hence. While I waited for it to get dark I sat listening to the owls in the wood at the top of the hill behind my house, and in a queer way I felt that they were a link between those paleolithic and neolithic times that were gone and that other stone age that was coming. They just survived our age, and the cities that were creeping away from London over the hills, and the need that commerce had for the trees in which they nested and hunted, and they survived the great flash that I saw and the radioactive snow, for I heard them again through the futuroscope when the woods came back again. How many survived the flash and the snow that followed I do not know, but I think rather more then men. However, I am only guessing, for I did not see enough men for adequate calculations. Once I heard an owl calling in London and I will hardly be believed when I say it, but it almost seemed to me like a warning voice to tell me that Man with his cities was going the wrong way; and that was before I had even heard of a futuroscope and had no way whatever of knowing what was coming. Of course I dismissed the idea as absurd, and yet I remembered it. And now I was listening to owls again, and they reminded me of the forests and ancient things and wilder things than Man, by which I mean the men that we know today. Then one more hoot seemed to remind me that it was time to go and see what that little neolithic band with their paleolithic ally were going to do in the forest of the Weald.

I knew they would do nothing till it was quite dark, but now it was time to look for them. So I turned the futuroscope on and there was the forest, for I had left the place-knob just inside its edge, where the six men had gone in under the oaks, and I turned it the way they had gone. But in the dark of the forest I could not find them, so I ran the place-knob up and down for a bit, and still I could not find them all among the dim shadows, from which I could not have distinguished them except by their movement, even if I had lighted on them. And then I ran the luminous disk over the forest, which as I have explained before, though itself a pale circle of light, does not give any light to the darkness, and with it I looked for the gypsies' campfires, which I knew could easily be picked up in the night. And very soon I saw their red embers glowing, and little golden flames rising up from them now and then and dancing upon them and making the shadows of oaks run through the forest. And I saw Kate sitting by one of the fires near the cart with two or three gypsy women beside her and the gypsy men sitting or standing a little way off in a sort of a circle round her, and they were all armed. Some information or a shrewd guess seemed to have warned these gypsies that Bert would make an attempt to rescue Kate, unless she were guarded like this. There seemed to me to be a very poor chance for the six men who were somewhere in the forest to get through all these gypsies and then to take Kate away with them.

And then, as I looked all over the camp, I saw Mrs. Smith sitting alone, just as Bob had said, brewing something over a fire in an iron pot that seemed to have come down all that way from our time in some treasury of the gypsies. It was dark enough now for any attempt at a raid, but I still saw no sign of Joe and his sons or the old archer or the Wild Man, and everything was silent in the forest except for the owls, which were calling there as here. I swept the disk of the futuroscope wide round the camp, and still could see no shadows anywhere near it that were not the shadows of oaks. And then it occurred to me that all I had to do was to go on sweeping the disk round and round the camp until I saw shadows moving, and that would be them. So I moved it round and round outside the camp and, though I only saw darkness dimly illumined by starlight, and a blacker darkness amongst it which was the trunks of oaks, I still saw nothing that moved. Then I brought the disk in nearer to the camp where the light of the small fires reached out to the trunks of the oak-trees, making a circle through which I felt sure that nothing could pass unseen. Round and round I moved it and still saw nothing there, nor did I hear any sound of men except for certain merry notes that now and then skirled up from Lee's pipe and fell into silence again. From this monotonous circling I turned to look again at the camp, and nothing had altered there. Kate still sat by the fire with a rather hopeless look on her face, and three gypsy women were gazing into the fire and pretending not to watch her. The gypsy men all round her leaned nonchalantly against trees or sat on the ground, and were as watchful as the three women. Mrs. Smith still sat alone by her fire, brewing something which from her furtive air I thought that the others were not allowed to see. I wondered what it was. I took another circle round the camp and then turned back to look at the brew. And Mrs. Smith was gone.

There had been no cry from her, and so sudden was her disappearance that not only I did not see what happened, but none of the gypsies had seen it either and they still remained watching Kate. I ran the disk round and round the camp again, and then I saw a shadow move, which was either Bert or Joe. And then I saw the Wild Man with Mrs. Smith under his left arm and his right hand over her mouth and his two sticks clutched in his left hand; and I wondered how he did it with his left arm holding the witch, but they trailed behind him and seemed to give him no trouble, and Mrs. Smith seemed to be no burden to him either, for she was not struggling and evidently knew well that she was beaten. I saw six shadows moving swiftly and quietly away, and then I ran the disk back to the gypsies' camp to see if the little band was safe from pursuit. And still the gypsies had not moved. Kate, who was watching nobody, seemed with a quick look to notice first that Mrs. Smith had gone, and those who were watching her noticed that look and then they saw for themselves. One call one of the women gave, and when it was not answered they all knew what had happened. All was commotion then, but they could not tell in what direction the raiders were gone, and I could see, as they looked at Kate and then at the forest, that they knew that if they searched among all those oaks they might lose their captive. And they saw the dark of the forest all round them holding its secrets, secrets they knew too well from their years of wandering that the forest does not lightly give up at night. From me also the forest darkly preserved its secrets, and I saw no more of the raiders that night or the woman that they had captured.

Chapter XXX

I got up very late next morning, for I had been up much of the night, and after I had finished my breakfast I felt that the time was come to devote myself by means of the futuroscope to some study that would be of scientific interest; and so I connected it up with the mains and began to take some note of the flowers and birds and insects that in that far future time had survived whatever had been so bad for our cities. But I made no study of these things for long, for I found I could not tear my interest away from the people with whom by now it had become so much involved, and I merely switched the luminous disk once more on to the hut by the Darenth, and found, as I had expected, that they were all back there, with the exception of the Wild Man, who perhaps found their civilization, if such he called it, too intricate for him, and the timbers and the fireplace of their house, their pots and pans and the skins that they wore, too artificial for him. With them was Mrs. Smith, and Toby lay at the door. The old gypsy woman had no hope of escape, I saw that in her face rather than in the precautions of Joe's family and their dog. I heard them speak of the Wild Man, whose name I gathered was Loom, at least to them, though whether he used a name or not I did not know. It appeared from their talk that he had only recently come up from Sussex and stolen Liza and made his house with her in what is to us the property of the Southeastern Railway Company, and to this home he had now returned. I saw Bert turn to Mrs. Smith and ask her something about the future. And she drew out at once the crystal that she kept in wrappings amongst her clothes and looked into it and began speaking in a low voice, and what she said I could not hear. But I saw Bert shaking his head. And then he said, "Look into the crystal again."

So she looked again. And I saw that Bert was dissatisfied with the future she saw and wished her to foretell some other kind of future, and Mrs. Smith made no resistance and looked again and was about to foretell something more, when the doorbell rang and I had to go and answer it, and there stood an inspector, who had come about my licence for what he called my television set. A futuroscope I should explain needs an aerial very similar to the one in use for all television sets, and he must have seen the one on my roof. I had already made up my mind that argument would be useless and had decided to pay the licence, though I could not help defending myself when he asked me why I had not taken out the licence before. I said it was not exactly a television set; but unfortunately Mrs. Smith was speaking louder now, and he could hear her voice from the door.

"You have friends in there?" he said, taking a half step back and pretending to be ready to go away so as not to disturb me and my friends. But he knew perfectly well that the voice was in the nature of wireless, though of course he couldn't know what. If he had known what it really was, he would have seen that I was not liable to be dunned for a licence. But of course I could not make him understand that. Indeed it might have been hard to make anybody see exactly what the thing was, because at present, and as far as I know, it is unique, and they would have nothing to go by. I asked him to come into the room, and showed him the set, so that he could see that, as I had told him, it was not an ordinary television set. But he asked to be allowed to look through it, and of course he saw the hut, and I gave a slight touch to the knob so that he could look at the landscape.

"I see," he said. "A nature story."

"But not exactly television," I said rather lamely.

"Well, it isn't *here*," he said.

And there he was wrong, for he was looking right at the view that you can see from this window at which I am sitting now, sometimes writing these notes and sometimes turning to look at the future through the curious instrument which stands beside me. But he couldn't see that. It was nearly all hidden in forest.

"So it isn't here" was his final argument. And final arguments are not always right, but one sometimes has to give in to them. You cannot prove to a man what he cannot see; and the futuroscope is really a very complicated instrument, and not only that but I couldn't explain all the working of it myself. I couldn't even explain my wireless set, though I had much more time to get used to it. So when he said "It isn't here," he meant that the picture must come from over there, from a long way off, from Alexandra Palace or from anywhere. And that of course made it a television set in his eyes, and, for all I know, in the eyes of the law. So I paid. He gave me the receipt with a good deal of care, handing it to me with what looked like extra politeness; but somehow I felt all the time that he was handing it to me, though I cannot say why or how, that he was emphasizing to me that this receipt should have been earned by me several weeks ago. However it was, we parted without any more being said, and no proceedings have been taken. Then when the inspector had gone I switched off the futuroscope, not so much because he had taken up some of my time and I had other things to attend to, but rather because he was one of the noises and irks of the twentieth century, whose clamours make themselves so much felt that it is hard for one's interests to dwell in any other age. Many men do let their interests play in some distant age, when they collect antiques, for instance, or read a book or see a play on television, but sudden noises and cares or the need to answer the telephone can easily call them back, and this inspector with his questions, his demands and his receipt had called mine back and they dwelt here among us all, and for all the rest of that day I forgot Bert and Kate and Mrs. Smith and her crystal.

But at night, when the wind was in the woods like a sea, and the owls were calling out of it from the hill at the back of my house, and no sounds were coming up from this age of ours which it did not share with the ages, and it might have been any century, then I thought of them all again; I thought of Bert with his prisoner, and wondered if Kate would be safe with the gypsies, and tried to guess the future for both of them. So next morning, even before I had my breakfast, I turned on the futuroscope again and looked into the hut, and there they all were and Mrs. Smith sitting among them, and Toby lying across the doorway still. The sound-knob in this strange instrument does not give so strong a current as the other two, either the time-knob or the place-knob; or, to put it another way, I can see more clearly than hear through it. So I looked first at Mrs. Smith's face. And I saw a yearning in it, and her eyes were far from the walls of that hut, though Bert stood near her and looked as if he had been but recently speaking to her, but she did not seem to see him or any there. A look had come on her face that made me think of a swallow in an English cage when Spain is calling, or a cuckoo caught by an Arab of some North African mountains when it feels the lure of our hills, and I felt sure that the love of wandering, the yearning for the road through the forest, had come on the gypsy woman and she knew she must go.

Then Bert spoke to her again and she turned that far gaze back to him as though she had forgotten him and only remembered him after a while. Then she answered him, but I did not hear what she said, and again I saw him shaking his head. And then he said to her:

"Look into the crystal again, Mother of the gypsies."

And she looked again and gave a sigh, and I think that liberty and the lure of the road were too strong for her, and if Bert and Toby held the keys of these things she must give up even the future to them. For she looked into her crystal again and, speaking louder now, so that I heard every word, she said:

"I seem to see you and Kate at the Old Stones."

"Be sure, Mother of the gypsies," said Bert.

And she sighed again.

"Yes," she said, "I see you both clearly now."

Chapter XXXI

Mrs. Smith had only been captive a day and a night, but now with the shining of another day her resistance seemed to be broken. For clearly she had been resisting Bert's demands, which could have been none other than that the gypsies should give up Kate. But the road was calling her, and neither Kate nor all the treasure that the gypsies might have hoarded could keep her or them from the road. One night between stationary walls was enough. That morning she looked out at the valley through the open door that Toby guarded, and saw that it was fair enough; none would appreciate that better than a gypsy; but the world was fair and she would see it. Some are born to be students, some to wander. A gypsy in a house or in any one spot for many days was to a wanderer what reading one page of a book day after day would be to a student. There was wandering in her blood, and she must wander. So I saw that, whatever their terms, their captive would accept them. I had not yet had breakfast and I hurried to get it, but I always left the place-knob right on that hut and returned to look at it again and again all that morning to see what was going to happen. Mrs. Smith sat talking to Maud beside the embers of a small fire, while the men went about various work outside, except for the old archer, who probably remained in the hut to see that Mrs. Smith did not escape, though Maud and her Toby would have been quite enough for that. I do not know how many times I turned the futuroscope on and off again while nothing was happening. And then Bert came into the hut and asked her straight out if she would bring back Kate, and the old gypsy woman nodded her head and gave some sort of a smile, and Bert called Toby away from the door and said to Mrs. Smith, "Then you may go free."

She stood up at once and smiled again, and I shouted out, "Don't trust her!" I shouted it at the top of my voice, but I realized, the moment that I had done it, that not a whisper of what I had said could go down all those ages, and I realized how silly it was for me to have shouted, and I don't know what my cook thought. But Bert did not need my advice, even if I could have given it him; for he said, "You will return with her?"

"Oh yes," she answered, smiling again.

"Then leave your crystal ball," said Bert, "and you will find it when you return."

"The crystal ball!" she gasped.

And I knew from the tone of her voice that this was the orb and crown and sceptre of the gypsies.

I switched off then, for I no longer felt any uneasiness about the old gypsy witch's return. She had no modern conveniences, no wireless set, no television and no futuroscope: the crystal was all she had for any glimpse at the future; to lose it would be to have closed the only window from which she could have looked at the years to be, and when it was closed each one of her tribe would know it, and she would be no more than an ordinary gypsy; and I knew that the old woman would never abdicate.

Nor did she. Had she had to choose between liberty and being queen of the gypsies she must have chosen liberty, for without that she could not be a gypsy at all; without the road and the forest she would have been a mere neolithic savage or a dweller in a city's flat, according to what age she inhabited, and I do not know which she would have detested most; probably both equally, as the Greeks called all foreigners barbarians, because the languages of all of them sounded equally to be bar bar bar. But this was not the choice before Mrs. Smith now; she had only to leave her crystal ball in the hut until she went to the camp of her tribe and returned, as a king might put aside the Great Seal for a day. So she had liberty and the road, without which she could not live; and before her tribe found out that she was not carrying the orb of the gypsies she would be a queen again. She smiled no more, but rose and nodded her head and put the crystal down on the beechen table and walked out of the hut.

I did not follow her, for I knew that she would go to her tribe's encampment as straight as a queen bee goes to its hive. How she would find it I did not trouble to think. I knew that Mrs. Smith would know the way. I ran the luminous disk instead beyond the Old Stones and under the oaks of the Weald and hunted about among them to find the gypsies' encampment, for I was anxious to see if Kate was safe. And after a long while I picked up one wheel-track on a golden patch of sand, which had been thrust up through the flowers as though a gnome mining for fairy gold had thrown a handful up. And after that it was easy, I came soon on their pony grazing, and their cart with its shafts on the ground, and fires lit and the women cooking. And there was Kate sitting upon the bracken, leaning against a tree, and Lee near her playing his pipe, and Kate's head turned away from him to where some thrushes were singing. The other gypsy men were not interfering with Kate, but they were as before, at various points which made roughly a circle round her, and very bright eyes watched her from where the children were playing. Nor was she ever out of sight of two or three gypsy women. Besides being at convenient points from which to watch against any attempt to rescue Kate most of the gypsy men seemed to be setting snares for rabbits and a few of the women were skinning some that they had already caught. And I was glad to see that rabbits, like some of our own descendants, had survived the cleverness of scientific man. I listened for a while with my luminous disk in the pleasant gloom of the forest that was lit by shafts of sunlight here and there which come dazzling down on to moss and other bright things, and by flashes of leaping flame that shone from the fires of the gypsies, but once I had seen that Kate was safe I had nothing more to keep me in the forest; for, charmed though I was with that idyllic scene to which Nature had returned after so much exile, I had things to attend to in my own house and there with a flick of my finger I returned. I had plenty of time in which to attend to them and to have my lunch in comfort, because Mrs. Smith had what would seem to us a long way to go to get to the Old Stones, and some way further than that to pick up her tribe in the forest, and there was nothing more that I particularly wanted to watch until she got there, when I was anxious to see whether she had the authority to take Kate from Lee. Perhaps, I thought, they might have some way of finding out that she no longer carried the crystal ball and, if they did, I thought that her authority might wane with that discovery. And then I fancied that Lee might keep Kate after all.

But it is not of my thoughts and fancies that I have any wish to write, but only of what I saw in the futuroscope, and all the purpose of these notes is only to indicate what it can show. I allowed Mrs. Smith four miles an hour for her journey, and I did not think she would do less, and I estimated the journey as something like sixteen miles. So the moment I had finished my lunch I went to the futuroscope again, and in a few moments I was six hundred years away, where Nature reigned over the Weald. And there was the gypsy pony grazing, and

Kate sitting disconsolate under the same tree, and Lee still piping as though he had no other way in which to waste the afternoon, and Kate still looking as though she did not care how he wasted it, and only a little way off I saw Mrs. Smith approaching. How would the gypsies meet this new attack, I wondered? For they guarded Kate, and whoever took her from them must surely be regarded as a raider. How much was Mrs. Smith's authority over them I did not know. And now she came in sight of the camp and Kate looked up, but without interest. And Lee went on piping. She walked through the cordon of men that were setting snares, and went up to Kate. Nobody spoke. Mrs. Smith took Kate by the wrist and walked away.

Chapter XXXII

I draw near the end of my story, which arose out of my desire to exhibit to the public the pleasures of a futuroscope, and which unfortunately has led me far away from my purpose, which was purely a scientific one. Had I serious qualifications to undertake any scientific study, the fascination of the subject would have undoubtedly held me to it, and I should never have wandered away to any story of the trivial affairs of a crudely simple people; but, lacking these qualifications, I have allowed that simple interest to grip mine, and my only excuse is that those interests of theirs, though simple, were so ardent, that my own interest seemed unable to escape from them, and I have found myself, ever more and more since first I looked into the futuroscope, paying more attention to the hopes and fancies of such people as Bert and Kate than I have to the payment of bills, the purchase of groceries, and one thing and another in my small house; and in the larger world, who won the lawn-tennis finals or cleared most on the football pools.

And it was the same again this evening when I had more important things to attend to, trivial things in themselves, but particles, even though minute, of the progress across this planet of a very wonderful age; and instead of paying proper attention to them I switched on that futuroscope again, and turning the place-knob to Local, I watched the Darenth valley towards the southeast to look for the return of Kate. For of one thing I was certain, that Mrs. Smith would waste no time, even by resting on the way, before she should get back to her crystal ball. What she saw in it I do not know: all that mattered was what she pretended to see in it, and what she and the gypsies saw in that pretence. For I think she must have seen in it all she pretended to see, because without that she would have hardly had the force to impose her visions on the rest of the gypsies, as she certainly had done. For she dominated that tribe, as I could see, not only because she was the mother of many of them: men can forget that; the Masai, for instance, when their mothers get too old put them out in the forest for the lion; and even the Kikuyus, who are not so harsh as to do that, cut a hole in the wall of the hut near her bed when the mother gets too old so that the lion or the hyena can put in his head and drag her away. Nor let us be too critical of them for that; for till not so long ago our own countrymen designated certain numbers of old women as witches and treated them no better than the old women of the Kikuyus and Masai are treated. It was not, then, as the mother and grandmother of so many gypsies that Mrs. Smith held her power, but as the possessor of a mystery, the crystal ball, which in its crude and simple way undertook work not so dissimilar to that which has been perfected in the futuroscope.

Bert was doing exactly what I was doing, wasting his time watching. Neither of us could bring Kate any nearer by looking up the valley for her, neither of us could hasten Mrs. Smith. Yet we were both doing the same thing, merely gazing. Six hundred years apart we were sharing one impatience, with at the back of Bert's mind, I am sure, the same futile thought which was at the back of mine, that by going on gazing we would see Kate sooner, and that the sooner we saw her the sooner she would be there. Muddled thoughts, maybe, but without them should we not lose all our modern verse? So I sat gazing up the valley, and Bert gazed the same way. Why did he not go to meet her, I thought, among other idle thoughts that came to me that afternoon, when I had nothing else to do but to play with such thoughts as I sat at my window here with my eye to the futuroscope, which was lighting up for me this valley six hundred years hence, this valley in which I live now. And then among other such thoughts the idea came to me that Bert would know that Mrs. Smith would never give up Kate till her crystal ball was restored to her. Could not Bert have taken it with him, I thought then? But no, they would guard that orb and treasure of the gypsies in the hut and expose it to no risk. It was the ransom of Kate. We went on gazing, Bert and I, and still saw nothing. Perhaps we had both overestimated, not the fierce vigour of Mrs. Smith, but the power it had over her limbs when they were tired with age and the long journey and responded sluggishly to the commands of that fierce spirit. Not that thirty miles or so would seem long to Bert; but, if he knew that gypsies grew old, he might not have known the check that age can put on their strides.

So he waited and wondered just as I did, and it was not till pigeons were beginning to drop in to the forests, and the shadows were all down the slope of the western hill, that I saw two figures coming our way from the Weald. That they were Mrs. Smith and Kate I was sure at once, and when I saw that one of them was still gripping the other by the wrist I knew I was right. Bert saw them at the same moment, and I could see from the glow in his face that he recognized Kate as soon as he saw her. He ran forward to meet her, and again that rather silly feeling came over me that I was eavesdropping. Of course I was eavesdropping; what else is the futuroscope for? Or television, for that matter? And there was no need to be ashamed of it. But I was, and I drew the light away and turned it into the hut. There I waited for the return of Kate and for Mrs. Smith's recapture of the crystal ball that gave her her power over the gypsies and which spread an awe, or at least a certain wonder, among some who dwelt beyond the gypsies' encampments. And presently she and Kate and Bert came in, and I saw in the old gypsy's eyes, as she looked at her crystal ball lying upon its scarves on the long table, the same glow that I had seen in the eyes of Bert when he first saw Kate in the distance. She reached out a lean hand, Maud nodded her head, and Mrs. Smith had hold of her crystal again.

"Look in it, mother of the gypsies," said Bert to her. And Mrs. Smith looked. She gazed at it like a poet seeing a vision, led by an inspiration that has deserted him for a while. Bert's arm was resting upon Kate's shoulders. "What do you see for us?" he said.

"What I told you," said Mrs. Smith.

"Tell us again," he said.

"I see you and Kate at the Old Stones," she said. "I see you in three days time. She is wearing thyme in her hair and the wandering flower."

I do not know what she meant by the wandering flower, but I thought of convolvulus.

"And she has a garland of clematis. I see you walking together seven times round the Old Stones, which is a symbol of eternity."

And I do not know what she meant by this either; but then I knew nothing of their rites, and could only guess.

"And I see the Seer of Canterbury standing by the eastern stone and blessing you. And my people are there too, even Lee."

And all this I saw too, three days later, when I went with my luminous disk to the Old Stones, and there they all were just as she had said. The gypsy people sat a little way off, none of them coming so close to the Old Stones as to leave the shadow of the oaks of their own country, which the forest was to them, and among whose mysteries they felt safer than within the area of whatever magic slept, and sometimes awoke, in that old grey circle. Liza was there with an apron full of the petals of rose-willow, with which she was strewing the path round the mound of the Old Stones along which Bert and Kate were to walk, just as Mrs. Smith had said she saw in the crystal. And other girls were there, whom I had never seen before, girls from huts whose smoke I had sometimes seen rise from the forest, but of whom I knew nothing. They too had aprons full of rose-willow and went round that path with Liza, strewing it till it glowed with the intense pink of that lovely flower. And then behind them came Kate with Bert, and I saw the Seer of Canterbury stand by the eastern end of the circle, where the three or four stones form a little roofless room whose fourth side opens towards the dawn. And it was at dawn that I saw all this.

They began their procession round the Old Stones as the sun looked over the hill, the girls strewing rose-willow and Bert and Kate walking behind. And, as far as I could make out, the Seer of Canterbury was blessing them as they went, seven times, as the old gypsy woman had said. But I knew nothing of their ceremonies, and what it all signified I cannot say. A purple glow of thyme was on Kate's head and a wreath of convolvulus, and she wore a garland of clematis, one mass of bloom, all of which Mrs. Smith had seen in the crystal, but, for all I know, these flowers may all have been part of some ritual that Mrs. Smith would have known without having to look in a crystal. And that

I cannot say, or she may have herself helped to attire the girl, fulfilling her own prophecy. And she wore many necklaces besides, all of strung harebells lit by a great chain of mulleins, and she carried a bouquet just as they do now, one great mass of scented orchids and pyramid orchids in the centre. All the girls who were scattering flowers were adorned with flowers too, and not only wild flowers, though with foxgloves and scabious and mulleins they were gorgeous enough, but hollyhocks and other flowers of our gardens that had gone wild like men and women and had survived the flash and the snow.

The ceremony being meaningless to me I cannot describe it clearly or even fairly, but it was beautiful with all those flowers, which seemed to smile like the girls all the more brightly for the dark background of the grim memories that slept in the old grey stones. Liza and all the girls wore many bright ornaments besides their wreaths of flowers, for Mother Earth can give many adornments besides jewels: necklaces of brilliant sea-shells were shining on all of them, and shells from the chalk hills, and brooches and pendants made of the hedge-sparrows' eggs, and some had crystals flashing in their hair, hewed from the heart of a flint. But on none of them was there any piece of metal, except among the gypsies. When the gypsies first saw the Seer walk into the stone circle, wearing the sharp curved knife of flint at his belt which he always wore, they shrunk a little away and their circle widened right back to the trunks of the oaks, but they did not go, and remained seated watching. I saw Lee there and wondered what he would do, and to my surprise he looked unconcerned. Then he drew out his pipe and began to play, and it was as though the merriment in the tune beat back to his heart, and his dark face wreathed with smiles. On the ground was something that he kept beside him, which at first I could not see; every now and then he bent over it and seemed carefully to be completing something that he had made, and every now and then he went on with his piping again. The Wild Man I did not see. If he had come with Liza, he now lurked out of my sight in the forest and mingled neither with the gypsies nor with Kate's people, and, much as this savage man was feared, I think he may have feared all who were not as savage as him, perhaps dreading that he might be caught up in a system which led to he knew not what and that he would no longer be free. I did not look for him in the forest, for all my interest was rivetted on the circle of old stones, in which the Seer stood alone, and on the procession of girls strewing flowers, and Bert and Kate walking round the flower-strewn path seven times. And then the girls all sang some chant or song, whose words I could not catch, and even the gypsies joined in from under the oaks.

It was a strange ceremony, of which I could make neither head nor tail; but they all seemed happy, and that was the chief thing. When they left the Old Stones in procession, the girls that had strewn the flowers dancing in front, and then Bert and Kate, the Seer stood and blessed them as they went, even the gypsies, for the gypsies followed some way too, led by Lee quite merrily playing his pipe. And then I saw what he had had beside him on the grass, it was something of the nature of a mandoline that he had made and which was now strung by a leather strap over his shoulder. I followed the procession some way, but when the chalk downs came in sight and they left the oaks of the Weald the gypsies came no farther. And then Lee put his pipe away and took from his shoulders his new mandoline, raw and crude enough to my eyes, but full of an enchantment to him that I could not see; and he played on it and lifted his head and walked towards the forest, and I saw that with this new weapon that could war with spirits and bring them to surrender, as a sword wars with bodies, he felt that the future was his and that he was invincible.

I followed the procession a long way, and then went home to my breakfast, for I had been up since dawn. It will be understood of course that when I say I went home I turned my eyes from the futuroscope and walked into the next room, where my breakfast was waiting; but the gathering up of my fascinated interest from six hundred years away and bringing back my attention to such a different valley as the one that I see from my window in such a different age is something more than a walk of half a dozen yards. One's eyes blink and one's mind readjusts itself and one searches all among one's little possessions, trying to find out which are essential and which are likely to be washed away by the first wave of a tide of time. Breakfast at any rate was essential, and I had that. And some while afterwards I went back to look at the procession and found them still coming this way, that is to say towards the North downs out of the Weald, the girls before Bert and Kate singing and dancing. I ran the disk on ahead of them then, to look at the entrance to the tunnel above Twitton, in which Liza and the Wild Man had made their home. Neither of them was there, and I went in to look; I mean I turned the luminous disk into the entrance; and I found the tunnel was much tidier then it had been; skins were neatly hung up, bracken was laid down for bedding, there was no rubbish lying about; but if I start describing all the details of the tidiness made by a woman's hand in any dwelling, I shall find too much for my pen. For a moment I ran the time-knob on many years, keeping the place-knob still, and I found Liza's family in that tunnel, now made neater yet, children of all ages, and I wondered which way they would go. Would they, and their children, remain paleolithic, or would they go Liza's way? And, if they did, would they remain what she was, practically neolithic? Or would they go on, generation by generation, to what the Wild Man dreaded, to the white collar again, of which his instincts had warned him, and clerks working indoors all day or keeping a shop in Sussex, perhaps in a rebuilt London? Who knows? All this I decided to investigate, and would have done so, but for what I have still to tell.

I took another glance at the bridal procession, to see what way it was going. Indeed, I kept in touch with them most of the morning with many such glances, till I saw them go over the hills that frame this valley, through the wood in which Joe and his sons had fought the wolves, out on to those slopes that see the flash of the lake which fills much of the great London crater. And there, not far from Bob's hut, I saw a hut apparently newly built, small, but with many timbers stacked on the ground beside it, from which I guessed that Bert and any who helped him would build it gradually larger, probably with the speed with which we construct prefabs. They had chosen a spot by which a wild rose grew and a rambling thicket of honeysuckle, some tendrils of which had already been fastened with wooden pins to a wall, and I saw that by next year honeysuckle and roses would be all over the hut. There the procession left Bert and Kate, singing to them one farewell chant. And though I have not the pen of the writers of old who told their tales of those who lived happily ever after, yet one thing I had till lately which none of them ever had, and when I say that Bert and Kate lived happily ever after I say what I have actually seen with my eyes by one swift turn of the time-knob through several years. More than that I would have done to watch their future, though it was all golden as far as I saw, on that lovely hill-slope, and Liza's strange family and their families and their destiny I would have watched too, but for one thing. One day Methery asked for his futuroscope back.

Printed in the United States
34114LVS00003B/103-120